P9-CCP-177

Books by Laura Levine

THIS PEN FOR HIRE

LAST WRITES

KILLER BLONDE

SHOES TO DIE FOR

THE PMS MURDER

DEATH BY PANTYHOSE

CANDY CANE MURDER

KILLING BRIDEZILLA

KILLER CRUISE

DEATH OF A TROPHY WIFE

GINGERBREAD COOKIE MURDER

PAMPERED TO DEATH

DEATH OF A NEIGHBORHOOD WITCH

KILLING CUPID

DEATH BY TIARA

MURDER HAS NINE LIVES

DEATH OF A BACHELORETTE

DEATH OF A NEIGHBORHOOD SCROOGE

DEATH OF A GIGOLO

CHRISTMAS SWEETS

MURDER GETS A MAKEOVER

Published by Kensington Publishing Corp.

A Jaine Austen Mystery

DEATH OF A GIGOLO

LAURA LEVINE

KENSINGTON
PUBLISHING CORP.

www.kensingtonbooks.com

KENSINGTON BOOKS are published by

Kensington Publishing Corp.
119 West 40th Street
New York, NY 10018

Copyright © 2019 by Laura Levine

All Kensington Titles, Imprints, and Distributed Lines are available at special quantity discounts for bulk purchases for sales promotions, premiums, fund-raising, and educational or institutional use. Special book excerpts or customized printings can also be created to fit specific needs. For details, write or phone the office of the Kensington special sales manager: Kensington Publishing Corp119 West 40th Street, New York, NY 10018, attn: Special Sales Department, Phone: 1-800-221-2647.

The K logo is a trademark of Kensington Publishing Corp.

ISBN-13: 978-1-4967-0853-3
ISBN-10: 1-4967-0853-9
First Kensington Hardcover Edition: October 2019
First Kensington Mass Market Edition: January 2021

ISBN-13: 978-1-4967-0854-0 (ebook)
ISBN-10: 1-4967-0854-7 (ebook)

10 9 8 7 6 5 4 3 2 1

Printed in the United States of America

Prologue

The Los Angeles morning fog was rolling in, thick as whipped cream on a Mocha Frappuccino. But inside my bedroom it was bright and sunny, a Technicolor world with Disney bluebirds chirping at my shoulders.

The reason for all this sunshine and light?

I'm thrilled to report that Cupid, who'd been snubbing me for years, had suddenly come flying into my life, pinging me with his arrow of love.

Thanks to the wonders of Internet dating, I'd reconnected with my ex-husband, formerly known as The Blob, now known as the Most Wonderful Man in the World. Or, as it appeared on his driver's license, Dickie Elliott.

True, our marriage had been a disaster—littered with forgotten birthdays, serial unemployment, and toenail clippings in the kitchen sink. (His, not mine.)

But over the years we'd been apart, Dickie had changed.

Gone was the slacker in flip-flops, rooted to the sofa watching *Beavis and Butt-Head* reruns. My former Dufus Royale now had a steady job as a graphic artist and a condo in Venice with a spectacular view of the Pacific.

I'd been seeing him for a while (six weeks, three days, and fourteen and a half hours—but who's counting?), and had rediscovered the sweet, sensitive artist I'd fallen in love with when I'd first met him.

Yes, Cupid was certainly zinging his arrow my way, and for that I was supremely grateful.

I was lying in bed that morning, Cinderella in a Got Chocolate? sleep tee, trying to ignore my cat, Prozac, clawing me for her breakfast, when my cell phone buzzed.

Eagerly, I reached for it.

"Morning, sweetie."

Do you hear angels singing? I did. It was *him*!

"See you tonight?" he asked, his voice like warm velvet.

"My place at seven," I managed to say after my heart stopped ricocheting in my chest.

"Miss you," he cooed.

"Miss you more."

"No, miss *you* more."

"No, miss *you* more."

"No, miss *you*—"

By now Prozac was thumping her tail in disgust.

Any more of this goo, I'm gonna hurl a hairball.

After a volley of kissy noises with Dickie, I hung up to face Prozac's wrath.

Sad to say, my kitty was not on board my love train. She sensed that this was something serious. And she didn't like it. Not one bit. No way was she about to relinquish her title as my Significant Other.

I'd tried my best to explain to her that there was plenty of room in my heart for her *and* Dickie, but she was having none of it. Every time he stopped by my apartment, she was a hissing, scratching bundle of hostility.

But I didn't have time to worry about Prozac. I had to shower and dress for a very important job interview.

Yes, it seemed that love had entered my life in more ways than one. That very morning I was headed off to apply for a job co-authoring a romance novel!

My neighbor, Lance Venable, who, as a shoe salesman at Neiman Marcus, fondles the tootsies of the one-per-centers, had set me up with one of his mega-wealthy customers, a would-be romance novelist by the name of Daisy Kincaid.

Admittedly I had zero qualifications to write a romance novel, having spent the past several years writing ads for low-rent clients like Toiletmasters Plumbers (*In a Rush to Flush? Call Toiletmasters!*), Fiedler on the Roof roofers, and Tip Top Cleaners (*We Clean For You! We Press For You! We Even Dye For You!*).

But the recent reappearance of Cupid in my life had inspired me to take on the challenge. (Not to mention the $10,000 Daisy was paying.)

I'd sent her a writing sample, a seven-page mini-romance I'd managed to dash off about a man and a woman in the same apartment building who fall in love when they keep getting each other's mail by mistake.

It wasn't exactly *Wuthering Heights*, but I thought it was cute. I only hoped Daisy would like it and offer me the job.

Breakfast duly scarfed down, I was gazing at a framed

photo of Dickie on my coffee table, daydreaming about my possible new life as a romance novelist—and, not incidentally, the whipped cream on a Mocha Frappuccino—when I realized if I didn't hurry I'd be late for my interview.

After a quickie shower, I popped into my official job interview outfit—skinny jeans, silk blouse, and blazer—accessorized with silver hoop earrings and my one and only pair of Manolo Blahniks.

A dash of lipstick, a crunch of my curls, and I was set to go.

"Wish me luck," I called out to Prozac as I grabbed my car keys.

But she was too busy hissing at Dickie's picture to even glance my way.

Chapter 1

The first thing I noticed as I drove up to Daisy Kincaid's estate was a brass plaque at the foot of her driveway, engraved with the words *LA BELLE VIE*.

Thanks to Mrs. Wallis, my French teacher at Hermosa High (*Bonjour*, Mme. Wallis!), I knew that *la belle vie* meant "beautiful life."

No kidding, I thought, as I wended my way up to Daisy's villa—a castle-like affair with arched colonnades, enough balconies to house a troupe of Rapunzels, and a gurgling fountain out front.

Think Downton Abbey with palm trees.

I parked in the circular gravel driveway, and after a quick inspection of my curls in my rearview mirror, I trotted over to ring the doorbell.

Deep chimes reverberated within the house, and seconds later, the front door was opened by a svelte young blonde, her hair coiled in a chignon. So elegant did she look that for an instant I thought she was Daisy Kincaid. But then I realized she was wearing a crisp, white maid's uniform.

"Ms. Austen?" she asked.

"That's me."

"Come right in. Ms. Kincaid is expecting you."

I followed her through a foyer the size of a hotel lobby into a living room littered with priceless bibelots and centuries-old antiques.

"Have a seat," she said. "Ms. Kincaid will be right with you."

With that, she left me to marvel at the gewgaws strewn around me. I was looking at the painting hanging over the fireplace (signed by a fellow named Picasso) when I smelled a blast of tea rose perfume.

I turned to see a short marshmallow of a woman with a wide smile and neon red pixie hairdo. She floated toward me in a turquoise caftan—turquoise necklace nestled in her ample bosom, turquoise bracelets jangling from her arms, and a honker of a turquoise ring on her pinkie.

"Jaine, dear," she trilled, extending her bejeweled hand. "So lovely to meet you. Do have a seat."

I parked my fanny on a sofa no doubt once owned by Louis XIV as Daisy plunked herself down on an equally posh armchair.

"Lance has told me so much about you! I can't believe you're the one who wrote *In a rush to flush? Call Toilet-masters*! I see it on bus benches all over town."

I put on my best aw shucks smile.

"And to think! You're an Emmy-winning TV writer, too."

Darn that Lance. He's always making up the most outrageous lies. True, I once worked on a long-forgotten TV sitcom and had another gig on an equally forgettable reality show, but the closest I ever came to an Emmy was seeing one on TV.

"I'm afraid I didn't really win an Emmy," I admitted, hoping it wasn't going to cost me the job. "Lance must have gotten his facts mixed up."

"Oh well. No matter," Daisy replied with a sweep of her turquoise sleeve. "I was very impressed by the little story you wrote. *Romance at the Mailbox*. So precious."

"I'm glad you liked it."

"Liked it? I loved it! I just know we're going to make a terrific writing team."

"Does that mean I get the job?"

"Indeed you do!"

Yes! I got the job!

"Do you want to hear my story idea?" she asked, eyes twinkling with excitement.

"Absolutely!"

"I'm calling it *Fifty Shades of Turquoise*!"

Whoa, Nelly. Suddenly I saw a Cease & Desist order from E. L. James's attorneys winging our way.

"Are you sure you can use that name? It's awfully similar to *Fifty Shades of Grey*."

"Oh, poo! Grey is so blah, and turquoise is so much more fun. I just adore the color!"

No surprise there, I thought, taking in her caftan, jewelry, and assorted turquoise throw pillows strewn among the antiques.

"Our book won't be at all like that dreary little grey series."

That only sold about a gazillion books.

"So what's the story line?" I asked, praying it didn't involve handcuffs and chains.

As luck would have it, it did not involve any handcuffs or chains.

In fact, it had no plot whatsoever.

"I haven't exactly worked out the details yet," Daisy confessed. "I thought you could do that. You'll sketch out the story, and I'll do the fine-tuning. All I know is that I want there to be a fifty-room mansion with every room painted a different shade of turquoise, and that somehow the heroine winds up making love to the hero in every one of those rooms."

Sex in fifty turquoise rooms? Suddenly my confidence as a romance writer plummeted. No way was I going to be able to write this bilge.

"So what do you think?" Daisy asked with an eager smile. "Are you on board?"

Absolutely not. I had to steer clear of this train wreck of a novel before it took off.

"As I told Lance," Daisy reminded me, "the salary will be ten thousand dollars."

"When do we start?"

What can I say? I've got the backbone of a Slurpee.

"Just sign right here," she said, whipping out a contract from the pocket of her caftan.

Thrilled to see all the zeroes on my salary, I signed on the dotted line.

"Let's start right now," Daisy said. "I hope you don't mind working here at the house. That way it will be easier for us to collaborate."

"I don't mind a bit," I assured her. Working there would be like working at the Four Seasons. Besides, I was getting tired of Prozac stomping on my keyboard in one of her anti-Dickie meltdowns.

Daisy led me to her office, a spacious room at the rear of the house—which I was relieved to see was not painted turquoise. Instead, it was bright white, with a wood beamed ceiling and French doors providing a breathtaking view of a pool and tennis court beyond.

One wall featured an ornately carved bookcase filled with thick, leather-bound volumes; another wall adorned with what looked like a genuine Renoir.

Two antique desks were face-to-face in the middle of the room, topped with twin laptops and Villeroy & Boch mugs filled to capacity with sharpened pencils. Seated at one of the desks was a sturdy thirtysomething gal with Harry Potter glasses and a mop of sandy hair even curlier than mine.

"Jaine, I'd like you to meet Kate, my personal assistant. You two will be sharing the office."

"Welcome aboard!" Kate said, shooting me a friendly smile.

"You can use my desk while you're working here," Daisy said. "And here's your laptop." She pointed to a shiny silver beauty on my desk. "I bought it especially for our little project."

Holy moly! The woman bought a brand-new computer for one file. I was in the land of the one-percenters, all right.

"I'd better scoot along now so you can get started."

And with a flash of her turquoise ring, Daisy waved good-bye and sailed out of the room.

The minute she was gone, Kate shot me a pitying gaze.

"So you're the poor soul who got saddled with *Fifty Shades of Turquoise*. What a clunker, huh?"

"It does seem a bit far-fetched," I said, trying to be tactful as I settled down at my desk.

"Oh, well. At least you're getting ten thousand bucks out of the deal."

I guess she could see the look of surprise on my face when she mentioned my salary, because she hastened to explain, "I do Daisy's books and keep track of all her expenses. So I pretty much know what she's paying for everything.

"Daisy's an utter doll to work for," she added, slinging her Nikes on her desk. "The pay is great, and rumor has it, she's left all her employees a generous chunk of change in her will."

Talk about your job perks.

"And as if all that weren't enough, the food's terrific, too. Raymond, her chef, used to work at some fancy French restaurant. And the freezer is stocked with Dove Bars, Eskimo Pies, and whatever flavor ice cream you like. My favorite is Chunky Monkey."

"You're kidding. So's mine!"

"It's a good thing I wear elastic waist pants," she said, "otherwise I'd never make it out of here alive."

"You wear elastic waist pants?"

Elastic waist pants just happen to be a staple of my wardrobe, second only to my CUCKOO FOR COCOA PUFFS T-shirts.

"Can't live without 'em."

"Me too!" I marveled. "It's unbelievable. Curly hair. Chunky Monkey. Elastic waist pants. I think we may have been separated at birth."

We spent the next several minutes chatting about curl definers, curl shapers, curl straighteners, and our mutual adulation of Ben & Jerry. I could've gone on yakking like this for hours, anything to avoid facing *Fifty Shades of Turquoise*, but Kate was made of sterner stuff.

"I'd better get back to work," she said. "Just ask if you need anything."

With no more diversionary tactics left, I opened a *Fifty Shades of Turquoise* file on Daisy's brand-new laptop and stared at the blank screen in front of me.

And kept on staring.

Not a single idea popped into my cranium.

Filled with a growing sense of panic, wondering how I was ever going to wrangle my heroine into fifty shades of turquoise lovemaking, my eyes wandered to a framed photo on my desk—of a middle-aged man in a business suit, with a toddler on his lap.

Kate looked up from her Excel spreadsheet and saw me staring at the photo.

"That's Daisy with her dad," she explained. "He died when Daisy was very young and left Daisy a fortune. From what I gather, her mom wasn't exactly a model parent, foisted her off on a bunch of nannies. When she was in her twenties, Daisy got married, but it was total bust, lasted less than a year. After that, she became a recluse."

"Daisy, a recluse?"

I couldn't picture the bubbly redhead I'd just met walled off from the world.

"I know. It's hard to believe, but for decades she lived with only a companion, dividing her time between her Connecticut mansion and her country home in Tuscany, never socializing and rarely leaving the house except for an occasional nature walk."

"What made her come out of her shell?" I asked, still boggled at this downer version of Daisy.

"A horrible accident." Kate grimaced. "On her last trip

to Tuscany, her companion was killed while hiking. Fell off a cliff on a mountain trail. Daisy told me that was a turning point in her life. It made her realize how fleeting life is, and how she was throwing hers away. So she came back to the States, determined to live life to the fullest. Moved to Los Angeles, started making friends and wearing a lot of turquoise."

What a story! If only I could think of something half as interesting for the book.

After a few minutes staring outside at the pool and wishing I were lying on one of the chaises, sipping margaritas with Dickie, I forced myself to return to the task at hand.

By the time the maid arrived to summon us to lunch, you'll be proud to learn I did manage to write something down:

Note to self: Buy margarita mix.

Chapter 2

By now the morning fog had burned off and, what with the sun shining its little heart out, lunch was being served at the pool.

"Daisy always invites me to join her for meals," Kate said as we made our way outside. "Like I told you, she's a doll to work for. And wait till you taste Raymond's chow. Yum!"

Out on the patio, Daisy sat at a glass-topped wrought iron table with matching wrought iron chairs—cushioned in turquoise, of course.

Seated at her side was a silver-haired gent somewhere in his sixties, dressed in tennis whites, his pot belly not quite concealed under his polo, skinny legs popping out from white shorts.

"That's Clayton," Kate whispered as we approached

the table. "Lives down the street. Daisy's gentleman caller. He's gaga over her."

Indeed, he seemed to be gazing at Daisy with the ardor of a geriatric Romeo.

"It was quite a match," he was saying. "I beat him all three sets. And he calls himself a tennis pro."

"Hello, girls!" Daisy said, catching sight of us. "Jaine, come meet my dear friend, Clayton Manning."

Clayton jumped up to take my hand, his face a deep (possibly carcinogenic) tan, etched with wrinkles, watery blue eyes startling against his leathery skin.

"A pleasure to meet you, my dear."

"Clayton was just telling me about his exploits on the tennis court," Daisy said as Kate and I took our seats. "He's such a good player."

"I'm always trying to get Daisy to hit a few balls, but I can't seem to talk her into it."

"It's a disgrace," Daisy said ruefully. "Here I've got a perfectly lovely tennis court"—she gestured to the court beyond the pool—"and I never use it. I much prefer my morning walks."

"That's how we met," Clayton said, beaming at the memory. "Daisy was out for her morning constitutional and I was getting my mail. I took one look at her and forgot all about the one million dollars I may or may not have won from Publishers Clearing House."

He shot Daisy another look of love, which she rewarded with a weak smile.

Somehow I got the impression that Daisy wasn't quite ready to play Juliet to Clayton's Romeo.

"Clayton, dear," she said, eager to steer the conversation away from love among the Aarpsters. "Jaine is helping me write my romance novel."

Helping her? What the what? I was writing the darn thing. That is, I would've been writing it if I could think of a plot.

"So how are you coming along?" Daisy asked eagerly.

"Great," I lied.

"Wonderful! I'll stop by at the end of the day and see what you've got so far."

Oh, hell. I was going to have to come up with something by the end of the day.

I was quickly distracted from the image of my blank computer screen, however, when Daisy's beautiful blond maid showed up, elegant in her white uniform, wheeling a trolley with our lunches.

"Solange, honey," Daisy said. "I forgot to ask. How did your audition go?" Then, turning to me, she added, "Solange is an aspiring actress."

So that explained what this stunner was doing wheeling food trolleys.

"Ms. Kincaid is so kind," Solange said. "She lets me take time off to go to auditions."

"Did you get the part?" Daisy asked.

Solange shook her head wistfully.

"Don't give up," Daisy said, patting her arm. "I just know one day I'm going to see you up on the big screen, and I'll be able to say, 'She used to make my bed!'"

Solange grinned and, turning to the trolley, announced: "Salmon *en croûte*."

At first, I was disappointed. I'm not much of a fish fan. But this salmon, I saw, as Solange placed my plate in front of me, was wrapped in a flaky pastry shell. And as far as I'm concerned, anything with the word "pastry" can't be all bad.

I took a bite, and suddenly I was in fish heaven. The stuff was deelish.

Kate hadn't been exaggerating when she raved about Daisy's chef.

I was busy inhaling my salmon, Clayton in the middle of a highly dubious story about beating Andre Agassi in a charity tennis match, when a regal gal with salt-and-pepper hair came sweeping out onto the patio in billowy palazzo pants and a chiffon blouse. In her hand, she held a newspaper.

"That's Esme Larkin," Kate whispered to me. "Daisy's BFF."

Clayton, ever the gentleman, jumped up and pulled out a nearby chair for our new guest.

"Daisy, darling!" Esme said, bending down to air-kiss her buddy. "So wonderful to see you. And you, too, Clayton!"

Clearly not as egalitarian as Daisy, she lobbed a brisk nod at Kate and a questioning glance at me.

"Esme," Daisy said, leaping into the breach, "this is Jaine Austen."

Esme's stone-gray eyes swept over me, suddenly intrigued.

"Any relation to the world-renowned author?" she asked.

"Afraid not."

"Pity," she said, instantly dismissing me as an object of interest.

"Jaine's helping me write my book," Daisy explained

"*Fifty Shades of Turquoise!*" Esme gushed. "Such a fabulous title. Absolutely delicious."

That last bit uttered while looking longingly at the salmon on our plates.

"Esme, hon," Daisy said, following her gaze, "have you eaten lunch?"

"Actually, no. I've had such a hectic morning."

"Let me get you some salmon."

"If it's not a bother."

"No bother at all."

Daisy pressed a button on an intercom at the table.

"One more salmon, please, Solange."

"Of course, ma'am." Solange's voice, laced with static, came out from the machine.

"I'm not really all that hungry," Esme said, "but I suppose I can force down a few bites. Meanwhile, darling, I've got wonderful news!"

With that, she waved the newspaper she'd been carrying, the *Bel Air Society News*, a glossy, tabloid-sized paper filled with pictures of rich people showing off their facelifts at charity galas.

"Here you are on the front page!" Esme squealed. "In an article about our benefit for the Animal Welfare League."

She held out the paper so we could all see it.

The headline read:

Daisy Kincaid Hosts Charity Fundraiser
at La Belle Vie

And indeed, there was a picture of Daisy holding a champagne glass.

A frown marred Daisy's face.

"Oh, dear. You know how I hate publicity. It's so showy. My father always believed in giving anonymously. He disapproved of people who gave only to see their names in print. You promised you wouldn't have any photographers at the event."

"But I didn't, darling. I shot this photo myself on my iPhone and couldn't resist sending it to the paper. You're not miffed at me, are you?"

She arranged her chiseled features into a look of remorse.

"Of course not, hon," Daisy said, her smile back in action. "I could never be miffed at you.

"Esme is chairman of the Bel Air Animal Welfare League," Daisy explained to me, "and is a positive saint to all those poor abandoned cats and dogs."

Somehow it was hard to picture this granite-faced gal as a saint.

"We couldn't do our work without you, Daisy," Esme said. "We'd be positively lost without your generous donations."

In the middle of this mutual admiration praisefest, Solange showed up with Esme's salmon.

She had no sooner put it down on the table than Esme swan dived into it. For someone who wasn't very hungry, she sure was packing it away.

Can't say as I blame her. I was practically licking my plate.

And dessert—a creamy chocolate mousse—was equally fabulicious.

At the end of the meal, Daisy's chef, a lithe ponytailed guy, came out onto the patio in his white chef's jacket.

"Was everything to your liking, ma'am?" he asked Daisy.

"Oh, Raymond. It was divine, as usual. You are, without doubt, an absolute genius in the kitchen."

He glowed under her praise.

And I had to agree.

With meals like this, maybe writing *Fifty Shades of Turquoise* wouldn't be so bad, after all.

FIFTY SHADES OF TURQUOISE
Outline

Clarissa Weatherly, a raven-haired beauty with mesmerizing emerald eyes, is a spoiled socialite, living the high life in New York, dabbling at her job in an art gallery, engaged to be married to a dashing English nobleman. Then suddenly her world falls apart when she gets the tragic news that her father has died. Even more tragic, he's gambled away nearly all his fortune, leaving her penniless.

Clarissa is devastated, especially at the thought of losing Weatherly Manor, the fifty-room mansion where she grew up in Colorado. The home that stores so many precious memories is now in foreclosure. The only thing that remains of her father's estate is his turquoise mine, which is on the brink of shutting down.

More devastation is headed Clarissa's way when she tells her British nobleman fiancé that she is now penniless and he breaks off their engagement.

Blinded by tears, yet determined to save her childhood home, she returns to Colorado to take over the reins of the turquoise mine and turn it into a profit-making venture.

Back home at the mine, she discovers a crooked foreman, who has been robbing her father blind. She fires him on the spot. Knowing nothing about mining, she must rely on MAX LAREDO, a burly miner with abs of steel, to help her save her busi-

ness. Accustomed to being treated like a princess
all her life, Clarissa is furious when Max bosses
her around and barks orders at her. She absolutely
hates this swaggering idiot! At least that's what
she tells herself. Underneath his swagger, she
senses a good man with a kind heart. Not to men-
tion those abs of steel. As they work together, side
by side, overcoming one obstacle after another,
she finds herself growing more and more attracted
to this rough-hewn rock of a man. Together, they
continue to work tirelessly, and at last, they do it!
They make enough money to buy back Clarissa's
childhood mansion! Weatherly Manor is saved!

Not only that, the mine is soon making money
hand over fist.

And before Clarissa knows it, Algernon, her for-
mer fiancé, shows up, begging her to take him back.

For a minute, she's tempted, but then she takes
a good look at him and sees him for the
moneygrubbing cad he is. She realizes at that mo-
ment that her true love is Max, the burly miner.

She finds him at the mine, and there among the
turquoise stones, they fall into each other's arms.
The first of many nights of bliss to come.

Clarissa marries Max and, after buying back
her fifty-room mansion, she has each room painted
a different shade of turquoise—and proceeds to
make love in every one of them with her studly
new hubby.

Okay, that's the bilge I dreamed up for Daisy.

I gave it to her to read at the end of the day and headed
home, praying she'd like it.

Chapter 3

Unlike Clarissa Weatherly's, my life was not a raging sex-a-thon.

Determined to play it safe and not rush into things, I'd put off having dipsy doodle with Dickie. Sure, we'd fooled around, but as yet, we hadn't gone the distance.

But tonight, I'd decided, was the night.

I'd invited Dickie over for a home cooked dinner (well, home cooked by my neighborhood Italian restaurant) of lasagna, antipasto salad, and tiramisu for dessert. Bolstered by a glass of Chianti or two, I planned on letting my reformed ex sweep me off to the bedroom to consummate our newly rekindled love.

After handing in my magnum opus to Daisy, I headed home to shower and dress—with a pit stop to pick up my Italian dinner.

Back at my apartment, I found Prozac sprawled on the sofa, luxuriating in her umpteenth nap of the day.

"Hi, sweetpea," I said, scratching her behind her ears.

She gazed up at me with a loving expression that could mean only one thing:

I smell lasagna. When do we eat?

I'd cut my pampered princess the tiniest sliver of lasagna and was just putting the rest in the oven to keep warm when my neighbor Lance came banging at my front door.

Lance and I share a modest duplex on the fringes of Beverly Hills, light years away from the megamansions north of Wilshire.

"Hey, hon," he said, sailing into my apartment in cut-offs and T-shirt, his tight blond curls moussed to perfection. "Want to grab dinner and a movie?"

"Not tonight, Lance. I'm seeing Dickie."

A look of disapproval flitted across his face.

"Again?"

"Yes, again. I've been seeing Dickie for the past six weeks, three days, and twenty-two and a half hours, give or take a second or two. And I'm not about to stop now."

He shook his head, tsking in disapproval.

"Jaine, honey, I don't want to rain on your parade, but have you forgotten all the misery that guy put you through when you were married? The forgotten birthdays? The chronic unemployment? And what about the time he gave you those used flowers for your anniversary?"

It's true. On our fourth—and final—anniversary, Dickie had given me a bouquet he'd picked from the neighbor's trash without even bothering to remove the accompanying card. (*Happy Bat Mitzvah, Kimberly!*)

That, in fact, had been the last straw, the final indignity that sent me scuttling off to see a divorce attorney.

But that was a long time ago. Things were different now.

"Dickie's changed," I insisted. "He's not the man he used to be."

"Nobody really changes, Jaine. Honestly," he said, taking my hands in his. "I think you're making a big mistake. I only want what's best for you."

But did he really? I wondered.

Sure, on the surface, Lance believed he was looking out for my best interests. But underneath his concern, I detected a mother lode of jealousy.

For years Lance and I had been wading together through a swamp of losers, searching for Mr. Right. Now I'd found my true love while he was still stuck kissing frogs.

So far, I hadn't confronted him with my suspicions. And I wasn't about to do it then. I had to get ready for my all-important date with Dickie.

"I know you care about me, Lance, but I promise I'll be fine. Now you've got to scoot so I can take a shower and get dressed."

"Okay," he said. "If you're sure you know what you're doing . . ."

"Trust me, Lance. I know what I'm doing."

A skeptical meow from Prozac.

She knows what she's doing like I know advanced calculus.

After gently shoving Lance out the door, I set the table (with actual cloth napkins instead of my usual stash of paper napkins from KFC) and raced off to prep for my night of passion.

In the shower, I loofahed my skin to a rosy glow. Thoroughly exfoliated, I slipped into a pair of skinny jeans; slouchy, pink V-neck sweater; and strappy leather sandals.

Then I slapped on some makeup and sprayed myself with some divine Jo Malone White Jasmine perfume I'd splurged on at Nordstrom. It had been worth the splurge. Dickie loved it and was always telling me how good I smelled.

Back in the living room, I twirled in front of Pro.

"How do I look?"

She gazed up at me through slitted eyes.

Like a woman about to cheat on her cat.

Was there no one in my life who supported me on this Dickie thing?

But I didn't have time to mope about my lack of moral support, because just then Dickie showed up on my doorstep, tall and lanky in tight jeans and a denim work shirt, highlights glistening in his sun-bleached hair, his soulful brown eyes burning with what I hoped was lust.

From her perch on the sofa, Prozac lobbed him a genial hiss.

"Hey there," he said, running his finger along my cheek. "You smell great."

Thank you, Jo Malone!

Then he pulled me into his arms for a steamroller of a kiss.

"Nice to see you, too," I managed to croak when we finally came up for air, my nether regions melting into a puddle of goo.

"I brought something for Prozac," he said.

Having been temporarily blinded by his tight jeans, I now realized he was carrying a squeaky toy mouse.

"Look what I got you, Prozac!" he said, tossing it to her.

She gazed at it disdainfully, then batted it away with the expertise of a World Series champ.

"Prozac!" I admonished her. "How could you?"

"No worries," Dickie said. "She'll get used to me in time."

An angry thump of Pro's tail.

Wanna bet?

After a few more steamy smooches, Dickie and I finally wrenched ourselves away from each other and settled down to dinner.

Normally, Pro shows up any time she's within pouncing distance of food. But that night she stayed firmly planted on the sofa, perfecting her hissing skills.

Aside from the hairball Dickie found in his napkin, dinner was dreamy.

I'd lowered the lights and lit candles to ramp up the romance.

And it was working.

Sipping our wine, we rubbed each other's arms and played footsie under the table, all the while chatting about our respective days.

Dickie told me about the project he was working on at his ad agency, and I told him about my new job with Daisy, confiding my fears about being able to write a romance novel.

That's the great thing about the new Dickie. The old Dickie would have jumped straight to "Jeez, I sure hope you don't get fired. We could use the money for a new power drill."

But the new Dickie—thanks to a guy named Hapi, a

new age guru he'd been studying with—was bubbling with affirmations and positive energy.

"Don't worry, Jaine," he reassured me. "I'm sure you'll do great. Just think good thoughts. Every time I feel challenged, I tell myself, 'I always find a way out of any problem life throws in my path.'"

A disgusted hiss from the sofa.

If only you could find a way out of this apartment.

We continued to scarf down our chow, me making a conscious effort not to inhale mine at my usual speed of light. I was sitting there trying to figure out which was yummier, Dickie's bod or the lasagna (Dickie's bod the clear winner), and thinking about the tiramisu I'd picked up for dessert, when Dickie dropped his bombshell.

"This lasagna's super, hon. I'm so impressed that you had the time to roll out the pasta yourself."

Okay, so I'd fibbed a little.

"But I'm afraid it's the last time I'll be eating it. I've decided to follow in Hapi's footsteps and become a vegetarian."

"No biggie. We can always eat meatless lasagna."

"It's more than that. In addition to meat, I'm giving up fats, glutens, and sugars."

Holy mackerel? What was there left to eat? Oh, well. To each his own, right?

And that's when he lowered the boom.

"I was hoping you'd give it a try, too. If we're going to be together, I want you to be at your healthy best. So what do you say?"

Was he kidding? No pizza? No fried chicken? No Quarter Pounders? No way!

But then he took my hand in his, and I felt an electric charge in my Happy Place.

"Sure," I said, in a lovestruck daze. "Why not?"

Obviously my hormones had taken control of my vocal cords.

"Wonderful!" he grinned.

With that, he pulled me up from my seat and folded me in his arms for another round of high-voltage smooching.

"What do you say," he murmured in my ear, "we skip the tiramisu and have dessert in the bedroom?"

What?? No tiramisu??

But, my hormones still raging, I wound up saying, "Yes. The bedroom. Now!"

Clinging together, we stumbled into my bedroom, specially spruced up for the occasion and spritzed with White Jasmine.

We flopped onto the bed and began tearing off each other's clothes with the kind of abandon that comes after six weeks, three days, and twenty-three and a half hours of abstinence.

Our lustfest screeched to a halt, however, when a furry ball of yowling rage came burrowing between us like a nun at a high school dance.

What the heck do you two think you're doing?

Furious, I scooped her off the bed and frog-marched her back to the living room, where I plopped her on the sofa.

She gave me her patented Abandoned Orphan look, yowling at the top of her lungs.

Okay, go ahead. Break my heart! Desert me for that gluten-free gasbag! Leave me alone and lonely with nothing but your favorite throw pillow to claw to shreds—

I left her mid-yowl and raced back to the bedroom, shutting the door firmly behind me.

I was ready to hurl myself into Dickie's arms when I noticed an ugly scratch along one of them—a farewell gift from Prozac, no doubt.

"Omigosh. you're bleeding! Can I get you some Bactine?"

"No, no," he said, ignoring his arm and pulling me to him. "I'm fine. Now that you're here."

The flame of our lust, I must admit, had been slightly dampened by Prozac's dramatic entrance, but now we were building up another head of steam. Things were just about to shift into All Systems Go when we were assailed by a fresh batch of yowls from Pro, scratching wildly at the bedroom door.

Dickie sighed and rolled over onto his back.

"I don't think this is going to work, Jaine."

"You're telling me!"

That last bit of wisdom from Lance, who can hear everything through our paper-thin walls.

"Next time," Dickie said, "let's meet up at my place."

"Good idea."

Again, from Lance.

Dickie threw on his clothes and, after a quick peck on my cheek, made his way past a hissing Prozac out my front door.

"I may never speak to you again," I said to Prozac as I watched Dickie walk down the path to his car. "You're in big trouble, young lady. Big trouble."

She yawned in boredom.

Yeah, right. Whatever. Now let's have some tiramisu.

There was no denying it. My cat was spoiled rotten. If things were going to work with me and Dickie, I had to stop being such a patsy and show her who was boss.

From now on, things were going to be different. I was going to be a tough cookie, a stern taskmaster, a strict disciplinarian.

And my new Show Prozac Who's Boss regime would start that very night.

Right after I gave her just the teensiest slice of tiramisu.

YOU'VE GOT MAIL!

To: Jausten
From: Shoptillyoudrop
Subject: Exciting News!

Hi, sweetheart!

Hope all is well with you and your precious cat, Zoloft.

Exciting news here in Florida. Lydia Pinkus, beloved president of the Tampa Vistas Homeowners Association, is organizing a sculpture class—to be taught by a local sculptor and owner of one of Tampa's most prestigious art galleries. I'm always so impressed with the way Lydia finds such fascinating things for us to do.

I can't wait to broaden my artistic horizons with this fun and stimulating class!

I tried to talk Daddy into going, but he absolutely refuses.

XOXO,
Mom

To: Jausten
From: DaddyO
Subject: A Gift from the Gods

Dearest Lambchop—Your mom's been yammering all morning about some stupid sculpture class Lydia "The Battle-Ax" Pinkus is organizing.

That's one class I won't be going to. As I always say, a day without Lydia Pinkus is a gift from the gods.

Love 'n snuggles from,
DaddyO

PS. Guess what came in the mail? A discount coupon for a $5 haircut. Now *that's* something to get excited about! I think I'll give it a try.

To: Jausten
From: Shoptillyoudrop
Subject: Cheating on Harvy

Daddy just went off to get a discount haircut. I can't believe he's "cheating" on Harvy, the stylist who's been cutting our hair for the past fifteen years. Harvy always does such a lovely job. But you know Daddy. He can't resist a bargain.

XOXO,
Mom

PS. I only hope Harvy doesn't find out about Daddy's betrayal. I once went to Supercuts for an emergency trim while Harvy was on vacation, and it took him three months to forgive me. Every time I called for an appointment he claimed he was booked. It was sheer agony until he finally relented and agreed to see me.

To: Jausten
From: Shoptillyoudrop
Subject: The Worst Haircut Ever!

OMG! Daddy just came back from the discount hair salon with the worst haircut ever! Not only did they dye his hair an Eddie Munster jet black, they tortured the few remaining hairs on the top of his head so they're standing straight up. I swear, he looks like a balding porcupine.

Worst of all, the whole thing is glued together with a ghastly hair "wax" that smells like bad fish.

XOXO,
Mom

PS. Between the cut, the blowout, and the dye job, that $5 haircut wound up costing $125!

To: Jausten
From: DaddyO
Subject: The Best Haircut Ever!

Just got back from Big Al's discount hair salon with the best haircut ever. A Metrosexual Mohawk that takes at least ten years off my life. All the stylists at the salon said I look fantastic.

And you should've seen the looks I got on the way home. People couldn't take their eyes off me.

What's more, Big Al gave me a complimentary jar of his special styling wax. Mom says it smells like bad fish, but I don't know what she's talking about. It has a delightfully tangy aroma, very mild. In fact, I can hardly smell it.

Love 'n hugs,
From your very stylish
DaddyO

Chapter 4

The good news: Daisy loved my outline.

"It's brilliant! Absolutely brilliant!" she'd gushed when I showed up for work the next morning, her eyes bright with excitement.

The bad news, of course, was that now I had to write the darn thing.

So there I was, alone in Daisy's office, Kate not yet in, staring at my blank computer screen.

How I wished I were writing about a Toiletmasters commode.

Do you realize how easy it is to write about a toilet bowl? All you have to do is dash off a few paragraphs about its sleek construction, double flush action, and optional built-in bidet, and you're done. A couple of hundred words at most.

But now I faced the daunting prospect of having to

churn out thousands and thousands of words about love in the turquoise mines.

I tried to think of a snazzy opening for Clarissa Weatherly's adventures but was coming up with zilch. I could practically see the tumbleweeds rolling in my brain.

So instead of concentrating on Clarissa, I checked my parents' emails, cringing at the thought of Daddy's smelly new hairdo.

As those of you familiar with my little sagas already know, my father—although a sweetie of the highest order—is a certified disaster magnet. The man attracts trouble like my thighs attract cellulite. It's so typical of Daddy to think he'd actually get a good haircut for five bucks. I just hoped he wouldn't drive Mom too crazy with his Metrosexual Mohawk.

After bidding my parents a fond cyber-adieu, I continued to perfect my work avoidance skills, resharpening the thirty-six already-sharpened pencils on my desk.

I was just taking the last one out of the sharpener when Kate breezed in.

Goodie! Someone to talk to! With any luck, I could keep this work avoidance thing going for another hour or two.

"Good morning," she said brightly, settling down across from me in her swivel chair. "How's it going? Do anything fun last night?"

"I was supposed to have a romantic evening with my boyfriend, but things didn't go exactly as planned."

"What a shame," she tsked. "I hope everything's okay with you two."

"Everything's fine. Just a furry blip on our radar screen."

"At least you have a boyfriend," she sighed.

"Not seeing anyone?"

"Only when I close my eyes and fantasize."

I felt her pain.

"The last guy I went out with asked me to dinner, didn't eat a thing, and spent the whole night licking Splenda from those little packets."

She groaned at the memory.

"Don't lose hope," I urged. "If I can find someone, so can you."

"I'm not so sure about that. All the funny, sensitive, good-looking guys already have boyfriends."

Six weeks ago, I would have agreed with her, but that was before Dickie made his grand re-entrance into my life.

Now I was happy. I was hopeful. I was filled with the wonder of romance.

If only I could get some of that wonder down on paper.

And then I thought of something that would give me the boost I needed. My favorite mental stimulant—chocolate!

"Want a Dove Bar?" I asked Kate, jumping up from my desk.

"Absolutely!"

And off I marched to the kitchen for our chocolate fix.

Daisy's kitchen was a cavernous room at the rear of the house, complete with a huge granite island, Sub-Zero fridge, six-burner stove, and restaurant-sized pantry.

As I approached the kitchen door, I heard a woman moaning. It sounded like Solange.

Gosh, I hoped she wasn't sick.

On the contrary. Solange was far from sick, I discovered as I swung open the door and saw her locked in an

X-rated embrace with Raymond, the chef. Her uniform was halfway unbuttoned, her hair freed from her chignon and flowing down past her shoulders.

The lovebirds sprang apart as I entered, Solange clutching her uniform to her chest to cover her exposed boob-age.

"So sorry to interrupt," I said.

"That's okay," Solange replied, her eyes still glazed over from her smoochfest.

Raymond put his arm around the pretty maid and squeezed her waist.

"As you can see, Solange and I are an item."

How lucky they were not to have Prozac in their lives, gumming up the works.

Instead, they had me.

"I was just coming to get a couple of Dove Bars."

"Help yourself," said Raymond, pointing to the huge Sub-Zero fridge.

But before I could get to the fridge, the doorbell rang.

"Damn!" Solange said, running her fingers through her love-mussed hair. "I can't answer the door like this."

"No worries," I said. "I'll do it."

"Would you? Thanks a bunch."

Leaving her to button up, I scooted off to the grand foyer to open the front door.

It was then that I got my first glimpse of Tommy LaSalle.

He stood on the doorstep in jeans, work boots, and a construction worker's vest, a tool belt slung around his hips. Tall and tan, with black hair and lake-blue eyes, he was an absolute stunner.

"Hello," he said, flashing me a smile meant to enchant.

But there was something off-putting about his smile. It

was the kind of calculated smile you see on used car salesmen and *Bachelorette* contestants.

"I'm here to see Daisy Kincaid," he said.

I wondered if Daisy was planning some remodeling. If so, I couldn't imagine what on earth she wanted to improve. Everything was already so perfect at La Belle Vie.

"I'll go get her," I said.

But I didn't have to go get her, because just then she came drifting down the stairs in one of her gauzy caftans.

"Jaine, sweetie! I was just coming to chat with you about *Fifty Shades*."

Then she caught sight of the stunner in the foyer and blinked at him questioningly.

"May I help you?"

"Mrs. Kincaid," the stunner said, "I hope you don't mind my stopping by. I saw your picture in the local paper while I was working on a construction job down the street."

From his back pocket, he pulled out a folded-up copy of the *Bel Air Society News*, the one with Daisy on the front page hosting her charity fund-raiser.

"If you're here for a charitable donation, you're going to have to talk to my personal assistant."

"No, no. I don't want any money," he said, with a meant-to-be endearing grin. "I'm Tommy LaSalle. My aunt Emma used to work for you as your companion."

"Good heavens!" Daisy cried, her hands flying up to her cheeks. "Emma's nephew!"

She beamed up at him.

"How lovely to meet you!"

"Aunt Emma always said such wonderful things about you. I wanted to stop by and thank you for the many kindnesses you showed her."

By now, Daisy's eyes were welling with tears.

"Poor, sweet Emma. I still can't believe she's gone."

I remembered Kate's tale about the loyal companion who'd died in a hiking accident in Tuscany, the companion whose death inspired Daisy to embark on a whole new life.

Daisy grabbed her hunky visitor by the hand. "You must stay so we can chat. Jaine, dear, tell Solange to bring us tea in the study.

"Imagine!" she exclaimed, still beaming at Tommy. "Darling Emma's nephew! How wonderful it will be to share our memories of her."

I watched as she and the hunk walked off to the study, Tommy's tool belt bouncing against his hip. And suddenly an uneasy feeling washed over me.

Something told me this guy was bad news.

But I was wrong. Tommy was worse than bad news. He made bad news look like a picnic in Provence.

If I'd only known what poop was about to hit the fan, I would've never opened the door to him in the first place.

Chapter 5

I grabbed some Dove Bars from the freezer, but sad to say, the chocolatey treat was not the fount of inspiration I'd hoped it would be. The minutes slogged by like centuries as I struggled to bring Clarissa Weatherly to life.

Really, she was a most uncooperative heroine.

I'd just managed to grind out three measly paragraphs when Solange put me out of my misery and summoned us to lunch.

Once again, our midday meal was being served out on the patio, and once again, Clayton was there when we showed up, pouring himself a glass of wine from a bottle cooling in an ice bucket.

Kate and I had just joined him when Daisy came sailing out, arm in arm with Tommy, her face wreathed in smiles.

"Everybody, I'd like you to meet Tommy LaSalle, my late companion Emma's nephew!"

As Daisy made introductions, Tommy barely glanced at me and Kate, dismissing us as the nobodies he thought we were. Then he turned to Clayton and nodded at him curtly, sizing up Daisy's ardent suitor, clearly finding him wanting.

Clayton, meanwhile, looked none too happy at the way Daisy's arm was linked so possessively in Tommy's.

"Clayton, sweetie," Daisy said, "would you mind scooting down a seat so Tommy can sit next to me? Now that I've found such an important link to my darling Emma, I can't bear to let him go."

Something told me darling Emma had nothing to do with the sparkle in Daisy's eyes.

Clayton grudgingly got up and moved down a seat.

"Wonderful news!" Daisy announced as she plopped down into her chair. "It turns out the lease has run out on Tommy's apartment and I've invited him to stay with me until he finds a new place!"

At this late-breaking bulletin, Clayton reached for his wineglass and took a healthy slug.

"So," he said, checking out Tommy's work clothes, "I take it you're a construction worker."

"Yep. Been doing it for the past five years. But I'm hoping to switch careers and make a move to financial planning."

"Don't you need a degree for that?" Clayton asked.

"Ordinarily, yes. But I'm sure I can make the transition. I've been playing the stock market on paper, and I've made a killing."

"It's easy to make a killing when you're not investing real money," Clayton said. "Playing the market takes a lot of skill. I should know. I used to be an investment banker. Trust me, young man. It's very hard work."

"I bet it was, sir, back in the days before they invented computers."

Clayton was sitting there, fuming at Tommy's snark attack, when Solange showed up, wheeling the lunch cart.

"Solange, dear!" Daisy said. "I need you to make up the blue guest room for Tommy. He'll be moving in with us."

"Yes, Mrs. Kinkaid," she said, blinking back her surprise.

"Tommy, you've already met Solange, our maid."

As Tommy smiled at Solange, I couldn't help but notice a flicker of interest in his eyes. A flicker that went undetected by Daisy, who'd been momentarily distracted by lunch.

"Mmm! Filet of sole meunière. How divine!"

And indeed it was. *Meunière* meant butter (as I knew from my high school French class—Thanks again, Mrs. Wallis!), and the fish was swimming in it. Like I said before, I'm not much of a fish eater, but this sole was dee-lish.

Tommy, however, was listlessly poking at his fish, unimpressed.

"Something wrong with your filet, Tommy?" Daisy asked.

"I'm afraid I don't go in for fancy French stuff. I'm more of a meat and potatoes kind of guy. I usually eat burgers for lunch. Or burritos. Or meatball subs."

"Why am I not surprised?" I heard Clayton mutter under his breath.

"A meatball sub!" Daisy chirped. "I've never had one of those. Sounds positively intriguing!"

Unnerved at the way Daisy was beaming at Tommy,

Clayton spoke up, making another valiant effort to defend his turf.

"I don't suppose you play tennis, Tommy. I'm guessing you're more into bowling and sports of that nature."

"Actually," Tommy volleyed back, "I play a little tennis. Learned when I was a kid at the Y."

"I'm senior division champ at the Bel Air Country Club," Clayton preened.

"Who gives a flying frisbee?"

Okay, what Tommy really said was, "Good for you." But there was no mistaking the disdain in his voice.

"You play tennis, Tommy?" Daisy chimed in. "How fascinating. I've always wanted to play but haven't had the time."

What the what? Just yesterday she was saying she had absolutely no interest in batting a ball around the court.

"We'll have to give it a shot, then," Tommy said, lobbing her his *Bachelorette* contestant smile.

By now, Clayton's face had turned an alarming shade of puce.

"Daisy, sweetheart," he said, emphasis on *sweetheart*, "I got the concert tickets."

Wrenching her eyes from Tommy, Daisy looked at Clayton in a daze.

"What concert?"

"Mozart at Disney Hall. This Saturday."

"Oh, right. How lovely." Then, like a magnet, her eyes snapped back to Tommy. "Do you like classical music, Tommy?"

"Not really," he confessed. "It's sorta dull. It always makes me sleepy."

"Me too!" Daisy giggled. "Aren't we just awful!"

At this final act of betrayal, Clayton grabbed his wine glass and slugged down the remaining contents in a single gulp.

The rest of the meal staggered along rather awkwardly as Clayton and Tommy traded barbed zingers, Daisy oblivious to the tension in the air.

To be honest, I was sort of oblivious myself, scarfing down my sole meunière. Really, I thought, as I shoved the stuff in my mouth, Raymond should be declared a national treasure.

After a spectacular dessert of flourless chocolate cake, Raymond came out to the patio in his chef's whites.

"Was everything to your liking?" he asked Daisy, just as he had the day before.

"It was very nice, Raymond," she replied with not nearly as much enthusiasm as she'd lavished on him yesterday. "But tomorrow, I think I'd like something less fancy. Like meatball subs."

"Meatball subs?" Raymond repeated, as if she'd just suggested serving Alpo on toast.

"Yes," Daisy nodded. "I think that would be a welcome change of pace."

Once again, she beamed at Tommy, gazing at him much like I gaze at a pepperoni pizza.

No doubt about it. My sixtysomething boss had the hots for her young houseguest.

The hunka hunka burning hots.

Chapter 6

Tommy moved in that afternoon, showing up in an Uber, his worldly possessions crammed into two Hefty bags.

Whatever he'd been hauling in those trash bags was quickly replaced in the ensuing days as Daisy took him on a whirlwind shopping spree, buying him Armani suits, Hugo Boss ties, handmade leather shoes, and two Rolexes—not to mention a boatload of athletic wear.

Daisy even converted one of the guest bedrooms on the main floor to a gym, complete with a rowing machine, treadmill, and a tanning bed to keep up Tommy's bronzed glow.

The gift Tommy seemed most taken with, however, was a platinum Swiss Army Knife, which he proudly used to clean the gunk from under his fingernails.

In return for all his new goodies, Tommy was showering Daisy with seductive smiles and glimpses of his six-pack abs. The job he really seemed to be applying for was Daisy's boy toy.

And it was working. The woman was utterly gaga over him, unable to tear her eyes away from his bod.

Unfortunately, she was alone in her ardor.

"I know a grifter when I see one," Kate confided when we got back from our first lunch with the tanned lothario. "And that guy is bad news."

She grew no fonder of him in the ensuing days when he started running her ragged, sending her all over town to pick up his favorite snacks—barbeque in Koreatown, dim sum from Monterey Park, and burritos from a Mexican food truck in Van Nuys.

"Who does he think I am?" Kate groused, exhausted from her freeway treks. "FedEx?"

Apparently so.

A few days after his arrival, he strolled into our office in cutoffs and a tank top, his thick mane of hair slicked back with gel.

"I'm in the mood for a chili cheese dog," he said to Kate. "Drive over to Pink's and get me one."

For those of you unfamiliar with L.A.'s restaurant scene, Pink's is a wildly popular hot dog stand at La Brea and Melrose—several light years away from Daisy's Bel Air manse.

Kate looked up from her computer screen and shot him a death ray glare.

"You expect me to drive all the way across town in traffic for a chili cheese dog?" she asked, furious at this latest request.

"With extra chili," Tommy replied, cleaning the gunk from his fingernails with his prized Swiss Army Knife. "So chop-chop. Better move your fanny."

Then, with a withering look at her tush, he added, "It could use the exercise."

Ouch. That had to hurt.

Kate got up and stomped over to him, her curls springing wildly from her head, as if outraged on her behalf.

"Sooner or later," Kate said through gritted teeth, "Daisy's going to realize what a sleazebag you are, and you'll be out of here so fast your head will be spinning."

"I wouldn't count on that, Tubby."

Tubby? That did it. Her face flushed with fury, Kate practically spat at him.

"You miserable fink!"

Okay, so "fink" wasn't the "F" word she used, but this is a family novel, so I'm keeping it clean.

I guess Tommy was used to being cursed at, because he barely batted an eye as he strolled out the room.

"And while you're at it," he called out, "get me a side of fries."

Kate wasn't the only one in the I Hate Tommy Club.

That afternoon, I wandered into the kitchen for a nice crisp apple (okay, apple turnover) and found Raymond chopping carrots with the ferocity of a samurai warrior.

"Tater Tots!" he groaned. "Two years at the Culinary Institute of America. Six years executive chef at Christophe, L.A.'s premiere French restaurant. And I'm reduced to serving Tater Tots." He eyed a plastic bag of the starchy offenders on the kitchen island and snarled, "Disgusting, no?"

I didn't have the heart to tell him I actually like Tater Tots. Preferably drenched in ketchup.

"Absolutely," I said instead, eager to soothe his frazzled nerves.

Next to Raymond, Solange was toiling at an ironing board, muttering curses as she worked.

"The nerve of that creep! Expecting me to iron his repulsive thong underwear."

She picked up a pair of freshly ironed leopard print thongs, gingerly holding them between the tips of two fingers.

"Ugh!"

Ugh, indeed. They looked like something you'd see in a porn flick. And I wouldn't have been at all surprised if they'd been in one.

"And he won't let me take time off to go to auditions," Solange fumed. "What a fathead!"

Once again, not the "F" word actually used.

Leaving the two of them to trash Tommy, I headed back to the office, grateful I'd not yet locked horns with Daisy's hunky heartthrob.

In fact, what with the excitement of Tommy's arrival, Daisy seemed to have forgotten about *Fifty Shades of Turquoise*.

The pressure was off!

Or so I thought.

Just when I figured I was off the hook, Daisy asked me

to send her the first few pages I'd written and summoned me to her bedroom to discuss the book.

I only hoped Tommy wouldn't be there to trash my work.

Daisy was alone, thank heavens, when I showed up at her bedroom—a pale turquoise affair dotted with priceless antiques no doubt mined from some castle on the Loire.

She was seated at her vanity in a vibrant floral silk caftan, screwing what looked like genuine emerald baguettes into her earlobes.

"Jaine, dear!" she cried, swinging around to face me. "I need to talk to you about our little book."

I braced myself for bad news. Surely she'd upchucked when she saw the glop I'd been writing about sinewy muscles, heaving bosoms, and loins of steel.

But there was no bad news.

"I've been so busy getting Tommy settled, I haven't had the chance to read what you've sent me."

I sent up a tiny prayer of thanks for my reprieve from the guillotine.

"But I've had the most wonderful idea," she beamed, "for Max Laredo, the burly miner Clarissa falls in love with. I know what I want him to look like. He should have black hair and blue eyes and a really deep tan."

Wow, I didn't have to be Sigmund F. to figure out that she wanted the leading man of her fictional romance to be the same as the leading man in her real-life romance.

"That's sound great," I lied, annoyed at the way Tommy had wormed his way into our book.

Daisy was busy applying mascara and gushing about how she just knew *Fifty Shades of Turquoise* was going to be a best seller, when we heard:

"Yoo hoo, Daisy, darling!"

It was Daisy's pal Esme, who came swooping into the room, decked out in yoga pants and hoodie, her salt-and-pepper hair swept back in a headband.

"Hello, sweetheart," she said, pecking Daisy on the cheek.

She nodded at me vaguely, dismissing me as social wallpaper.

"You're not wearing that beautiful silk caftan to the spa, are you?" she said, turning her attention back to Daisy.

"Oh, dear," Daisy said, dismayed. "Today's our spa day."

"Indeed it is!" Esme smiled.

"Don't be cross, Esme, but I'm afraid I forgot all about it. Tommy and I were planning to drive up the coast and have lunch in Malibu."

"That's too bad," Esme said, irritation flitting across her hawklike features. "Can't you go to Malibu another day?"

"Nope, she can't."

We turned to see Tommy looming in the doorway.

"She's having lunch with me," he said, striding to Daisy's side and clamping a possessive hand on her shoulder.

Esme's eyes narrowed into angry slits.

"You must be Tommy," she said, forcing a smile. "I'm Esme, Daisy's dearest friend."

"Not for long, bitch."

Okay, he didn't really say that, but I could practically see the cogs churning in his brain, trying to figure a way to oust Esme from Daisy's life.

"Tommy, dear," Daisy said, "would you mind awfully

if I went with Esme to the spa? We have a standing date every week, and I forgot all about it."

Esme smirked in victory. But she miscalculated her win a beat too soon.

"No problem," Tommy said, all oily compliance; "but I was really looking forward to a cozy lunch by the beach. Just the two of us."

That said with his finger grazing the nape of her neck.

"Okay, then," said Daisy said, eyes glazed, melting at his touch. "Lunch in Malibu it is."

Now it was Tommy's turn to smirk.

Seeing the disappointment on Esme's face, Daisy rushed to placate her.

"There's no reason for you to miss out on the spa, Esme. Wait right here, and I'll get you my membership card. I'm sure they'll let you in without me. Tell them to charge everything to my account."

As Daisy disappeared into her cavernous walk-in closet, Esme shot Tommy a withering look.

"Looks like someone won the lottery," she said, gazing at the Rolex on his wrist.

"Lucky me," Tommy replied, a poster boy for insolence.

"I heard on the grapevine you're a construction worker."

"You heard wrong. I'm not in that line of work anymore."

"I can tell exactly what line of work you're in," Esme sneered. "But don't you boys usually get paid by the hour for services rendered?"

Tommy looked like he was about to haul off and deck her when Daisy came bouncing back into the room, waving her spa membership card.

"Here it is!" she said, handing it to Esme. "Do you want Tommy's cell phone number in case you need to reach me in an emergency? You know how I'm always forgetting my cell."

"No need for that, hon," Esme replied. "I've already got Tommy's number."

Chalk up another member in the I Hate Tommy club.

Chapter 7

I hurried home from the cauldron of hostilities brewing at La Belle Vie, looking forward to the weekend ahead.

Dickie had been working late all week, so we hadn't had a chance to get together. But we'd kept in touch, texting and talking on the phone, and had set up plans to have a romantic dinner at his condo that night—followed by what I hoped would be a session of passionate dipsy doodle.

Back at my apartment, I luxuriated in the tub, fantasizing about what the night held in store—Prozac glaring down at me from her perch on my toilet tank.

I swear, that cat is psychic. She knew I was going to see Dickie, and she wasn't the least bit happy about it.

"I wish you'd give Dickie a chance, Pro. He's really a sweetie pie."

A disgusted thump of her tail.

Oh, please. If I have to listen to any more of his stupid affirmations, I'm putting myself up for adoption.

But I refused to let Prozac rain on my parade.

Studiously ignoring her dirty looks, I proceeded to get dressed, slap on my makeup, and crunch my curls so they were at their Botticelli best.

Then I headed out to my Corolla with a song in my heart, a smile on my face, and an extra spritz of perfume on my undies.

Dickie greeted me at the door of his Venice condo in jeans and a body-skimming polo, his sun-bleached hair provocatively spiky. Whisking me inside, he took me in his arms and hit me with a blockbuster of a kiss.

"Preview of coming attractions," he whispered in my ear.

Yikes. I only hoped I'd be able to hold out until after dinner.

I followed him into his hip, metrosexual living room— lots of dove-gray leather on dark hardwood floors, recessed lighting, and spotless white walls adorned with abstract art.

Back in the old days, Dickie's idea of fine art had been Elvis on velvet and *Dogs Playing Poker*.

"Let's watch the sunset," he said, leading me out onto his balcony with its spectacular view of the Pacific.

We settled down into twin chaises, sipping organic chardonnay and sharing a small plate of baby carrots.

Aside from the fact that there was no ranch dressing for the carrots, it was heaven.

Dickie began to tell me about his rough week at work, coming up with ideas for his new ad campaign. To tell the truth, I wasn't paying much attention, too busy staring at the tiny dimple in his cheek that flashed whenever he smiled.

"I'm just glad I had my spin class," he was saying. "What a great way to release tension."

Remembering the feel of his ripped bod as he held me in his arms, I was grateful for his spin class, too.

"And of course, I couldn't have made it through the week without one of Hapi's affirmations. I kept telling myself, *I am always prepared to dig in and do what is needed*."

"How inspirational," I said, wishing we had something more to eat than those darn carrots. Oh, well. A small sacrifice if it meant lounging next to my new and vastly improved ex-hubby.

After watching the sun set in a glorious orange ball, we went back inside for dinner—an appalling kale and tofu salad, accompanied by the merest speck of a gluten-free dinner roll.

But I didn't mind. Much.

At least there was no furry ball of fury nudging her way between us. I'd left Prozac sulking on the sofa, where she was no doubt at that very moment shredding one of my cashmere sweaters to ribbons.

"How's the chow?" Dickie asked.

"Yummy," I lied.

"I'm so glad you're sticking with Hapi's diet."

Dickie had emailed me Hapi's no fat/no fun diet earlier that week, with its rules about what I could eat (virtually nothing) and what I couldn't eat (virtually everything).

All of which I perused while scarfing down a bag of M&M's.

"If you feel yourself weakening, here's a great affirmation to keep you eating healthy: *I feel good only when I eat wholesome, natural food. I abhor junk food.*"

"I've got to remember that," I simpered, trying to look like a woman who abhorred junk food and not the kind of woman who kept an emergency carton of Chunky Monkey stashed in her freezer.

All this chatter about Hapi's diet was making me more than a tad uncomfy. So I was delighted when Dickie reached across the table and took my hand in his, an electric charge zipping through my bod.

"God, how've I missed you," Dickie moaned.

"Me, too!" I said, at last speaking the truth.

"You're so much more fun than Allison."

Wait. What? Who the heck was Allison?

"Allison?"

"My old girlfriend. We broke up right before you and I got together. She was very sweet but sort of dull. My heart just wasn't in it."

Whoa, Nelly. I had no idea he'd recently broken up with another woman.

"I felt the same way about Roger," I parried back. "He was a wonderful guy, and I loved being showered with gifts and swept off on weekend getaways to Santa Barbara, but in the end, I didn't feel a connection with him."

Of course, this was all doo doo of the highest order. There was no Roger. I just made him up so Dickie would have no idea of the vast wasteland formerly known as my love life.

If Dickie had an ex-girlfriend, I'd have an ex-boyfriend.

"Let's forget about Allison and Roger," Dickie said, gazing at me with what I hoped was lust in his luminous brown eyes.

And indeed it was. Because the next thing I knew, he'd scooped me up for another blockbuster kiss.

Soon we were stumbling off to his bedroom, our ghastly salads forgotten.

Undeterred by jealous felines, we hurled ourselves onto Dickie's California king bed. And, because my mom sometimes reads these little tales of mine, let's just say we spent the next hour "cuddling."

Twice.

Thank heavens the TV was off, no ESPN blaring in the background, as it used to when we were married, Dickie taking time out from sex to check the scores.

No, that night he was the perfect lover, the Dickie I remembered from our very first tryst. When we'd finished, we both lay back in his bed, slightly sweaty, still clinging to each other—me praying Dickie wouldn't take out his dental floss and begin flossing like he did on our honeymoon.

My prayers were answered. All he did, after a while, was kiss me on the forehead and ask me if I wanted some more wine.

He went off to get it, and when he was gone, instead of lying there, enjoying my post–dipsy doodle glow, I opened his night table drawer to see what he kept there.

I can't help it.

I'm a natural born snoop.

The minute I looked inside the drawer, however, I was sorry I did. My heart sank to see a framed picture of a stunning blonde. A perky beauty in shorts and a halter top, without an ounce of fat anywhere.

Was this "dull" Allison, Dickie's old girlfriend?

She sure didn't look very dull to me.

At first I told myself it was probably his sister, or a cousin. And then I remembered Dickie didn't have any sisters. And I'd met all his cousins at our wedding. None of them had been even remotely this hot.

What if this doll baby was Dickie's ex-girlfriend? And what if Dickie wasn't really over her? What if he still had the secret warmies for her?

Why else would he keep a picture of her in his night table?

I looked down at my naked bod and suddenly felt like a beached whale.

I made up my mind then and there to sign up for that spin class Dickie had been raving about and whittle myself down to a taut bikini-ready bod.

What's more, I'd get started on Hapi's ghastly diet.

Really. I would.

Just as soon as I finished that emergency carton of Chunky Monkey in my freezer.

Chapter 8

I woke up Monday morning in a post-Dickie glow. Although he had to work over the weekend during the day, we had the nights together.

Utter bliss.

Prozac, of course, was in major snit fit mode.

She sat on my bed, yowling in protest, as I got dressed.

I can't believe you abandoned me for two whole nights! What if I'd needed an emergency belly rub?

"Can the drama, Pro. Dickie and I could've stayed here if you weren't so awful to him."

An angry thump of her tail.

Dickie, Dickie, Dickie. That's all I ever hear around here. He may be cute, but can he poop in a slipper?

Normally I'd race to her side and stroke her until her snit fit was over. But not that morning. If I wanted things to work out with Dickie, it was time that cat got a much-needed dose of tough love.

Ignoring her yowls, I finished getting dressed, then grabbed my car keys and headed out the door without a shred of guilt.

Prozac's days of manipulating me were over.

I sailed off to La Belle Vie, happy snappy, energized by my weekend of dipsy doodle.

For the first time, I felt like I was making progress on *Fifty Shades of Turquoise*. Finally getting the hang of this romance thing, I was able to write about loins of steel and throbbing manhood without a barf bag on call.

I zipped through the pages, eating lunch at my desk, taking time out only to stab a few pins in a voodoo doll Kate had bought on Amazon.

She called it Voodoo Tommy (she'd even written his name across its chest with a Sharpie), and we both had great fun stabbing its throbbing manhood.

"If only I could do this to Tommy in real life," Kate sighed wistfully. "What fun that would be."

Tearing ourselves away from our castration hijinks, we got back to work.

Once again I was swept up in a tide of steamy romance as I chronicled the amorous adventures of Clarissa Weatherly.

When I finally checked the time, it was after six. Kate had long since gone. I packed up my things and was heading for the front door when Daisy called out to me from the living room.

Looking over, I saw her sitting on one of the two sofas flanking the fireplace—Tommy lounging next to her, picking his teeth with a doohickey on his Swiss Army Knife.

Esme and Clayton sat across from them on the other sofa as Solange and Raymond bustled about, serving hors d'oeuvres and pouring champagne.

"Jaine, dear!" Daisy said. "Won't you join us for cocktail hour?"

Wiped out from my day of purple passion, I just wanted to go home and have a nice long soak in the tub. But then my eyes glommed on to the serving platters, chockablock with Bagel Bites and—my favorite appetizer!—franks-in-a-blanket.

"Don't mind if I do," I said, hotfooting it over to the franks and nabbing one.

(Okay, two.)

After which I parked my fanny in one of Daisy's antique armchairs, hoping I wouldn't drop any pastry crumbs on the nosebleed-expensive upholstery.

"Are the Bagel Bites to your liking, sir?" Raymond asked Tommy, oozing contempt.

"Could be crispier," Tommy decreed.

Raymond opened his mouth to say something—a string of colorful curses, no doubt—but Solange shot him a warning glance, and he clamped his jaw shut.

Sensing her cook's ire, Daisy piped up, "The Bagel Bites are absolutely delicious, Raymond. A fun change of pace from your divine pate."

"Thank you, ma'am," Raymond said through gritted teeth.

When everyone had been served a glass of champagne, Solange asked, "Will that be all, ma'am?"

"No, don't go yet," Daisy replied. "I've got an important announcement to make."

She held up her champagne glass in a toast.

"Wonderful news! Tommy's found a job as a financial planner!"

Huh? This tooth-picking slacker actually landed a job?

"Who on earth hired him?" Esme asked, echoing my own skepticism.

"Me!" Daisy cried. "He's going to be my personal business manager."

Esme's eyes widened in disbelief.

"Have you lost your mind?"

Okay, so what she really said was "How nice," but it was clear she was royally gobsmacked.

"But he has no training in the field!" Clayton pointed out.

"True," Daisy said, "but Tommy's got a wonderful grasp of financial matters. Don't you, darling?" she added, turning to Tommy, gazing at him with undisguised longing.

"I don't like to toot my own horn," he said, "but I think Warren Buffett could learn a thing or two from me."

Puh-leese! What planet was this guy living on?

"Here's Tommy's new business card," Daisy said, jumping up and passing out thick, embossed cards, heralding Tommy as an "Executive Financial Planner."

"Best of all," she beamed, "Tommy will be staying here at La Belle Vie indefinitely."

Solange and Raymond gasped at this newsflash, exchanging looks of utter panic. Then they quickly excused themselves and hurried off, no doubt to update their résumés.

Esme managed a lame, "That's wonderful."

But Clayton didn't bother to hide his emotions. This young wiseass had just stolen Daisy out from under him.

He proceeded to give Tommy the royal stink eye as Daisy rattled on, oblivious.

"I'm thrilled Tommy's staying on," she was saying. "Now the home gym won't go to waste. I'm afraid I haven't been using it at all. I only wish you wouldn't spend so much time in that tanning bed, Tommy, dear."

She tore her eyes away from him to explain, "He's there like clockwork every morning at ten, tanning himself for twenty minutes. I worry he's overexposing himself to dangerous UV rays."

Clearly, she was the only one worried. Clayton and Esme seemed to be rooting for the UV rays. Especially Clayton, who looked as if he'd like nothing better than to see Tommy sprout a few skin cancers.

As for the newly minted financial whiz, he just sat there, blithely picking his teeth with that doohickey on his Swiss Army Knife.

"Must you pick your teeth like that?" Clayton finally snapped. "It's really most unappetizing, old chap."

"Old chap?" Tommy looked up lazily from the detritus on his toothpick. "I'm not the old one around here, buddy."

"Who are you calling old?" Clayton sputtered. "My doctor says I've got the body of a thirty-year-old."

"Better give it back," Tommy sneered. "You're getting it wrinkled."

By now, Clayton was practically foaming at the mouth.

"I'm not so old that I can't tan your hide in a tennis match."

At last, Tommy put down his toothpick.

"Really?" he said, a calculating gleam in his eye. "Why don't we play and find out?"

"You're on!" Clayton countered.

The two men glared at each other, battle lines drawn.

No doubt about it.

This meant war.

Chapter 9

I've never actually played tennis—way too much sweating, and not nearly enough thigh coverage—so I'm sort of hazy on the details. All I know is that Clayton and Tommy had decided to play what's known as a "set" of six games.

Tommy insisted that everyone attend.

As he put it, "I want an audience to watch me take down the old coot."

And so, if you'd been snooping around the grounds of La Belle Vie the next day at three PM, you would have found us all sitting in folding chairs alongside the tennis court: Daisy, Esme, Solange, Raymond, me, and Kate—who, just five minutes earlier, had been sticking pins in Voodoo Tommy's tennis arm.

Clayton, looking every inch the Silver Fox with his snowy mane of hair, showed up in spotless tennis whites with a state-of-the-art racquet.

Tommy, on the other hand, wore cutoff jeans and a tank top, brandishing a banged-up wooden racquet, probably from the sports equipment section of Goodwill.

He strutted out onto the tennis court, cockily bouncing a tennis ball.

"You're going down, old man," he called out across the net to Clayton.

Or so he thought.

Clayton, the pride of the Bel Air Country Club, opened fire with a smashing serve. Tommy raced to return it but missed by a mile.

A look of utter astonishment crossed his face. And stayed there throughout the game as Clayton took him to the cleaners, slamming balls over the net that Tommy, flailing about, failed to return.

"Poor Tommy," Daisy sighed. "I'm afraid he didn't realize how strong a player Clayton is."

The rest of us, of course, were grinning from ear to ear, thrilled at the sight of Tommy going down in defeat.

Next to me, Kate applauded wildly every time Clayton scored a point. If she could, she would have been in a cheerleader's outfit, waving a set of pom-poms.

"Daisy asked Tommy to be her financial planner?" she'd gasped when I told her the news. "What—Bozo the Clown wasn't available?"

On my other side, Raymond and Solange practically high-fived each other every time Tommy missed a ball.

"Eat dirt," I heard Raymond mutter, "you Bagel-Biting bastard!"

And so it went for the first two games, Tommy clearly outmatched by the silver-haired tennis maven.

But then, during the third game, things took a decided turn for the worse.

Tommy, who'd been standing around looking bewildered on the court, suddenly lost his awkwardness and started slamming balls over the net.

Clearly he was a good player. A very good player.

All those stumbles at the beginning were just an act; he'd been toying with Clayton, letting him believe he was going to win, waiting until the older man was tired before pulling out all his stops.

Now he had Clayton running ragged on the court.

"Too bad, old chap," Tommy sneered at Clayton whenever the Aarpster missed the ball.

The mood in the peanut gallery had turned from festive to funereal, everyone dismayed by this distressing turn of events.

Even Daisy looked upset.

"Oh dear. I'm afraid Clayton's no match for Tommy after all. I just hope he doesn't hurt himself."

I, too, feared for Clayton.

Sweating profusely, he looked like a prime candidate for a coronary.

At last Clayton was put out of his misery when Tommy scored his final point, winning the set. The two men approached the net to shake hands, Tommy bouncing a tennis ball in victory.

"Nice try, old chap," Tommy said, still bouncing the ball.

Fury blazed in Clayton's eyes.

"You may have won this set," he said, reaching over the net and snatching the ball from Tommy mid-bounce. "But our little game isn't over yet. Not by a long shot."

It looked like the war between Daisy's two suitors was still raging full throttle.

Chapter 10

Tommy swaggered into Daisy's office the next morning, flush from his victory on the tennis court.

Kate, who had been hard at work jabbing Voodoo Tommy in his erogenous zones, quickly shoved the doll in her desk drawer. Lucky for her, Tommy didn't see it, too busy admiring one of the Rolexes Daisy had given him—turning his wrist this way and that, watching the platinum gleam in the morning sun.

"What do you want now?" Kate asked, eyes narrowed. "Blintzes from Minsk? Crepes from Paris? Tamales from Tijuana?"

"I'm not here to see you," he said, finally tearing his eyes away from his wrist.

That could mean only one thing:

I was in the hot seat.

Sure enough, Tommy turned to me and said, "Daisy

wants to see Chapter One of your book. She's waiting for you in her bedroom."

And then he lowered the boom.

"She wants you to send me a copy, too. In case I have any suggestions."

Phooey. The last thing I needed was input from this Neanderthal.

"Send it to me at my business email," he said, tossing me one of the embossed business cards Daisy had handed out the other night.

"I can't believe I've got to show him my pages," I groaned after he sauntered off.

"Me, neither," Kate said. "I didn't know he could read."

With a sigh, I returned to Turquoise-Land and did a quick polish of Chapter One.

When I was through, I printed a copy for Daisy and sent off an attachment to Tommy.

"Wish me luck," I said to Kate as I headed off to see Daisy.

"You'll be fine," she assured me, retrieving Voodoo Tommy from her desk and resuming her stick pin torture.

Upstairs, I found Daisy at her vanity, dabbing lotion on her face. Propped up prominently on the vanity table was a picture of Daisy gazing lovestruck at Tommy, her chubby body nestled into his like a worn out pillow on a brand new mattress.

"Hi, Ms. Kincaid. I brought you those pages you wanted."

Daisy held up a hand, silencing me, and then motioned me to a nearby armchair.

What the heck was this all about? I wondered as I plunked myself down. Why was Daisy staring at her face in the mirror, stock still?

At last, she spoke.

"So sorry, honey. I have to keep my face perfectly still for sixty seconds after I use Insta-Lift."

"Insta-Lift?"

"A facelift in a jar!" she said, holding up a bottle of the lotion she'd been applying to her face. "Guaranteed to remove wrinkles for at least five hours."

And indeed, looking at her closely, I saw only faint traces of the laugh lines that normally animated her face. I couldn't help but be touched by her valiant attempt to breach the age gap between her and Tommy.

"You wanted to see the first chapter of *Fifty Shade of Turquoise*?" I asked, handing her the pages.

"Yes, I'm inviting Esme and Clayton over for tea so I can read it to them. I'm going to read them the whole book in installments as we write it."

We? I don't know if you're keeping track, but according to my lightning calculations, Daisy hadn't written Syllable One of our book.

"Won't that be fun?" Daisy gushed.

"Absolutely," I lied, dreading Clayton's reaction when he realized the sexy hero of the book was a thinly veiled version of Tommy.

"Tommy said you wanted him to take a look at the pages, too?" I asked, hoping her answer would a bewildered "No."

But alas, she was all on board with Tommy chucking in his two cents.

"Absolutely! Tommy has marvelous instincts!"

Yeah, right. Of a tenement rat.

"I'll give you a buzz as soon as I finish reading what you've written. I know it's going to be wonderful!"

And I left her applying Insta-Lift to the wrinkles on her cleavage.

I was more than a tad nervous when Tommy summoned me to the library later that afternoon.

Taking a deep breath, I headed into a wood-paneled room straight out of an English country manor—the walls lined with the same kind of thick leather-bound volumes that filled the bookcase in the office. Classics by Plato and Socrates, and *The Complete Works of William Shakespeare*. I couldn't picture Daisy actually reading this stuff. I figured some decorator picked them out because they matched the furniture.

Tommy looked up from where he was sprawled out on a tufted leather armchair, leafing through a Tiffany catalog. No doubt planning his next gift from Daisy.

"Grab a seat," he said, gesturing to a sofa across from him.

I sat down gingerly, wondering what havoc he was about to wreak on the first chapter of *Fifty Shades of Turquoise*.

"I read your pages," he said.

And?

He rolled his eyes in disgust.

"Gloppy, gooey, sugary pap."

Oh, crud.

"Daisy will love it."

Hallelujah! I was off the hook!

"And you're okay with it, too?" I asked.

"That depends."

I should've known there'd be a catch somewhere.

"I need you to write Daisy a love poem for me."

"A love poem?"

"Yeah, something sugary and stupid, like your book. You know. Stuff like 'When I look at you, my knees go weak, and my heart skips a beat.' Women eat that crap up."

Clearly he was trying to cement his relationship with Daisy with the kind of writing he knew she liked. I hated the thought of aiding and abetting this slimeball, but I hated the thought of rewriting Chapter One even more.

"You write the poem," he said, "and I'll like Chapter One. You good with that?"

"I'm good," I muttered.

"I thought you would be."

Then he looked me up and down appraisingly.

"What do you say we improvise a little romance scene of our own?"

The nerve of this guy! Coming on to me after he'd just asked me to write a love poem for Daisy.

"Are you nuts?" I asked, when I'd recovered my powers of speech.

"I know. It sounds crazy," Tommy said, "someone like me hooking up with someone like you. But I don't mind a gal with a little extra meat on her thighs."

"Yeah, well, I mind a guy with a little extra meat where his brain should be."

Of course, I didn't really say that.

Instead, I hauled myself out of there, wanting more than anything to whack him over the head with *The Complete Works of William Shakespeare*.

Chapter 11

For those of you wondering, I'm ashamed to admit I did not stick to Hapi's diet. Heck, I didn't even start it. One look at his suggested recipes—kale pudding, tofu casserole, turnip stew—had me running to my cupboard for emergency Oreos.

But that night I found myself in my kitchen, cutting zucchini into pasta-like strips for Hapi's zucchini "noodles" with eggplant and tomato. Dickie was stopping by for dinner, and I was not about to let him know what a diet scofflaw I'd been.

I'd invited him over to worm his way into Prozac's good graces, hoping that once Dickie gave her a few belly rubs and ear scratches, Prozac would be putty in his hands.

I was just opening a bottle of organic chardonnay when

Dickie showed up—looking *très* adorable in freshly ironed chinos and chambray work shirt, his arms laden with tulips for me and kitty treats for Prozac.

Back when we were married, the only thing he'd ever shown up with was beer on his breath.

"How're you doing, bunny face?" he said, putting down his gifts and wrapping me in his arms.

"Fine, now that you're here."

For that I was rewarded with a whopper of a kiss.

From her perch on the sofa, Prozac eyed us with disgust.

Puh-leese. Get a room.

Once I managed to pry myself from Dickie's arms, I put the tulips in a vase and we settled down for our zucchini "noodle" dinner—me telling the most outrageous lies about how much I was loving Hapi's draconian diet regime.

"I'm so proud of you, Jaine," Dickie said, taking my hand in his, my lady parts melting like cheese on the burgers I wished we were eating. "You know what I always say: Eat Hapi to Stay Healthy!"

A disgusted meow from Prozac.

Who is this Hapi guy, and why do I hate him so much?

"Remember, Jaine," Dickie said. "You've got to tell yourself every day: 'I only eat foods that are fresh and healthy.'"

Another meow from Pro.

I only eat foods that aren't nailed to the floor.

"Great advice!" I said, trying to sound as if I actually intended to follow it.

Much to my relief, Dickie stopped yakking about heal-

thy eating, and as we chatted about this and that, I somehow managed to choke down my zucchini noodles.

(Thanks heavens for that organic chardonnay!)

After dinner, we headed to the living room to start in
on Operation Wooing Prozac. As I told Dickie, the first
and foremost way to Prozac's heart is through her bot-
tomless stomach.

"Hold out one of the kitty treats," I instructed as we
made the perilous approach to the sofa.

At the sight of Dickie walking toward her, Prozac
bared her teeth in one of her more dramatic hisses.

"Did Roger have this much trouble with her?" Dickie
asked, beads of sweat beginning to pop up on his brow.

"Roger?"

"Your old boyfriend. The one you just broke up with."

Damn. I really had to keep better track of my fibs.

"Right. Roger. Yes, Prozac gave him a rough time. But
in the end, he won her over. And I know you can, too."

But Dickie didn't seem convinced. Looking more than
a tad intimidated, he held out a shaky hand.

"This is the hand I draw with. You sure this is safe?"

"You'll be fine," I promised with a confidence I did
not feel.

"Here, Prozac!" Dickie said. "Look what I've got for
you. A yummy treat!"

Prozac eyed him warily as he moved in toward her.

*If this idiot thinks he can win me over with a snack,
he's out of his mind, he's lost his marbles, he's—mmm, savory salmon innards!*

And just like that, she snapped the treat from his hand
and guzzled it down.

After which she looked up, impatient.

What are you waiting for, Hapi Boy? That salmon-flavored treat's not going to jump into my mouth by itself.

"She wants more!" I cried jubilantly. "This time, sit down next to her and feed it to her."

Dickie sat on the sofa and held out another treat in his hand.

Gone in a flash.

"Now try scratching her behind her ears!" I said, hovering nearby.

"You sure she won't claw me?"

"I doubt it," I said, watching Prozac as she curled up in a ball, belching salmon fumes. "She's in a post-snack stupor."

Dickie reached out to scratch her, and much to our joy, she let him.

But she still had that wary look in her eyes.

If this clown thinks I'm going to change my mind about him just because he's giving me a little scratch, he's got another think coming—Oh, Daddy! Higher! To the left! To the right. Now behind my tail. Aaaah!

Operation Wooing Prozac was working! Prozac was actually allowing Dickie to touch her—without bloodshed!

Emboldened by his success, Dickie scooped Prozac up into his lap, where she sat, purring.

"I think you've won her over!"

"I think I have," he said, flashing me a radiant smile. "As I learned from Hapi, I can overcome any hindrance and move past it with exuberance. I am a positive force in the universe."

He beamed with pride.

Down in his lap, however, Prozac's tail was thumping in an irritated staccato.

Never a good sign.

Another affirmation? That does it. The man's an idiot.

Without any further ado, Prozac leaped off Dickie's lap, and as she did, I was horrified to see a big wet stain on his crotch.

"Oh, hell!" Dickie cried, jumping up. "She peed in my lap!"

So much for Dickie's positive force in the universe.

Quickly he started unzipping his fly and taking off his pants.

In another time, another setting, I'd be thrilled.

Now I was just mortified. I raced to my closet and got him a pair of my sweats. Which I was even more mortified to see were too big around his waist.

Gaak! The new, improved Dickie had a waist smaller than mine!

"I'm so sorry about this," I said, as he picked up his stained chinos.

"Don't worry about it," he said. "These things take time."

But I could see a seed of doubt in his eyes.

And as he hurried out the door, I wondered how long he was going to put up with my cat from hell.

"Prozac Elizabeth Austen!" I cried the minute Dickie had gone. "I hope you're proud of yourself."

She gazed up at me, preening.

Very.

"I may never forgive you!"

You'll be happy to know I proceeded to give her the cold shoulder the rest of the night.

And by cold, I mean frigid.

In spite of her plaintive mews, there were no love scratches. No belly rubs. No salmon treats.

And if you think I gave her even a single slice of pepperoni from the pepperoni and sausage pizza I ordered after Dickie left, you're sadly mistaken.

Okay, so I gave her the sausage. But I didn't smile when I gave it to her. Which had to have hurt.

YOU'VE GOT MAIL!

To: Jausten
From: Shoptillyoudrop
Subject: The Death of Me Yet!

Daddy's Metrosexual Mohawk will be the death of me yet.

He keeps insisting that his hair wax has a tangy, manly smell, but I swear, that fishy goo can clear out a room faster than a bomb threat.

The other day we got on a long line at the supermarket, and one by one the people in front of us moved to another line! Today Edna Lindstrom sat down to join us at the clubhouse for lunch, and five minutes into the meal she had the waiter pack up her lunch to go. She claimed she had a headache, but I'm certain she couldn't stand one more minute of Daddy's stinky hair.

And you should see the looks Daddy has been getting. Like he's roadkill at a buffet table.

It's all so darn embarrassing!

XOXO,
Mom

To: Jausten
From: DaddyO
Subject: Smashing Success!

Well, Lambchop, I'm happy to report my new haircut is a smashing success. You should see the looks I've been getting! People are staring at me, awestruck!

And you won't believe the good luck this haircut has brought me. Ever since I got it, my life has been a breeze. No lines at the supermarket. Or the post office. And the other night at the movies, a tall guy sat down right in front of me and not two seconds later jumped up and changed seats.

Your mom keeps insisting that my hair smells like rotting fish, but frankly, I think she's just jealous of all the attention I've been getting.

Love 'n snuggles,
DaddyO

PS. I'm having such a good time showing off my new haircut, I've decided to sign up for The Battle-Ax's sculpting class and give the ladies a thrill.

To: Jausten
From: Shoptillyoudrop
Subject: Fooey!

Oh, fooey. Daddy's signed up for the sculpting class. I was hoping to escape from him and breathe some fresh air for a few hours.

To: Jausten
From: Shoptillyoudrop
Subject: What a Treat!

Just got back from our sculpture class. What a treat!
Our instructor, Molly—a darling young sprite of a
woman—was so sweet, so kind. I just know she's going
to be a wonderful teacher! I could see her wrinkle her
nose when Daddy walked in the studio, but she was
way too polite to say anything. Instead she sat him at a
station closest to an open window to dilute the stench
from his hair.

Molly urged us all to make something simple, like a
vase or a canape plate. But once Daddy learned that
Lydia, who has had prior sculpting experience, was
making a torso of Sir Isaac Newton, Daddy insisted on
making a replica of the Statue of Liberty. Molly tried to
talk him into doing something less challenging, but
Daddy was having none of it.

Daddy's always had an insane urge to compete with
Lydia. Every time he loses to her (and he always does),
he's convinced he's been a victim of foul play.

But enough about Daddy.

I'm making a canape plate, which will be winging its
way to you, honey, the minute it comes out of the kiln!
Perfect for one of your festive Los Angeles cocktail
parties!

XOXO,
Mom

To: Jausten
From: DaddyO
Subject: Babe Magnet

Back from sculpting class, Lambchop, where my new hairdo brought me good luck yet again! Our sculpting teacher, a very sweet young gal, gave me a prized seat right by a window.

And, like all the other ladies in the class, she couldn't seem to take her eyes off me. This new haircut of mine is a babe magnet. Of course, you know how much I love your mom and wouldn't dream of looking at another woman. But I must admit, it's a kick getting so much attention.

Most of the gals are making simple beginner projects, but not Lydia Pinkus, that world class show off. No, The Battle-Ax is making a bust of Sir Isaac Newton. Of course, hardly anybody knows what he actually looked like, so Lydia can get him all wrong and no one will know the difference. I'm sure she planned it that way.

Well, if she thinks she's going to get all the "oohs" and "aahs" in this class, she's sadly mistaken. I've decided to do a replica of the Statue of Liberty, certain to blow Lydia's stupid "Fig" Newton out of the water!

Love 'n hugs,
DaddyO

Chapter 12

Thank heavens Daisy liked Chapter One of *Fifty Shades of Turquoise*.

"Wonderful job, Jaine!" she cried, bustling into the office the next morning in her bathrobe, smelling of tea rose and Insta-Lift. "You must join us today when I read it to the others. Four o'clock, in the living room."

"I'll be there," I said.

I have to confess I was a wee bit nervous. Sure, Daisy liked my chapter. But she was really into this romance stuff. I just hoped Esme and Clayton would share her enthusiasm and I wouldn't get sent back to the drawing board.

"Well, I'm off!" Daisy said. "Must get dressed. Tommy and I are driving out to Malibu for lunch. We just love the sea air."

And off she sailed to prep for her date with Tommy.

Kate shuddered when I told her how Tommy had come on to me.

"Ugh!" She groaned. "What a sleazebag. I don't care how good looking he is, he'll always be repulsive to me."

By now she'd stuck so many pins in Voodoo Tommy, stuffing was beginning to pop out from the holes.

I spent the next hour grinding out Tommy's stupid love poem—an ode so gooey, I'm surprised the paper didn't stick to the printer when I printed it out.

But Tommy gave me a grudging "not bad" when I showed it to him in the library, where I found him leafing through a Bentley brochure.

"Thanks," I said, quickly scooting away before he could make another pass at me.

What with Daisy and Tommy off in Malibu, Kate and I ate lunch at our desks—scrumptious mushroom and gruyere cheese omelets. With just the tiniest sliver of flourless chocolate cake for dessert.

After plucking the last flourless crumbs from my plate, I checked my emails and groaned at the latest news from Tampa Vistas.

Poor Mom. Not only did she have to put up with Daddy's haircut from hell, now she had to sit by and watch another skirmish in Daddy's ongoing rivalry with his archenemy, Lydia Pinkus. So awkward for Mom, since Lydia is one of her BFFs.

But I couldn't fret about Mom, not with Clarissa Weatherly stomping her dainty feet in the wings.

By now, my plucky heroine had packed her bags and was headed off to find passion and profits in the turquoise mines. I pounded away on her saga until four PM, when it was time for tea.

Kate was out running errands for Tommy, so I was alone when I made my way down the back hallway. I was just about to step into the foyer when I heard voices. Peeking around the corner, I saw Esme staring at Tommy, slack-jawed.

"You've got to be kidding!" she was saying.

"Nope, dead serious," Tommy replied, clad in a crisp linen shirt and trousers, no doubt laboriously ironed by Solange. "I'm slashing Daisy's donation to your charity."

"But you can't!" Esme cried. "The Bel Air Animal Welfare League would be lost without Daisy's funding."

"Not my problem," Tommy drawled. "Now that I'm managing Daisy's finances, I've got other plans for how to spend her money."

"On yourself, no doubt."

"You know what they say," he smirked. "Charity begins at home."

"This is outrageous!" Esme fumed. "I can't believe Daisy would withdraw her support from such a worthy cause."

"You'd better believe it. She's already signed off on it. In case you haven't noticed, she's gaga over me. She'll do anything I want. I'm in charge here now."

"That's what you think, buddy," Esme snarled, eyes blazing. "I'm going to tell Daisy exactly what a lowlife you are and how you're just using her for her money."

"I wouldn't do that if I were you," Tommy said with a chilling smile. "Like I said, the old girl is crazy about me. I can promise you that if it's a contest between me and you, you're going down in flames."

And just like that, Esme caved.

She knew Tommy was right; there was no way she was going to win this battle.

Shoulders slumped in defeat, she headed into the living room.

Tommy strolled in after her with all the confidence of a man who knew he had Daisy Kincaid wrapped around his little finger.

After waiting a few judicious minutes, I made my way to the living room, where Tommy was lounging next to Daisy on one of the sofas, admiring his reflection in the blade of his Swiss Army Knife.

Clayton and Esme sat across from them, Esme still in shock over the financial blow her charity had just been dealt.

Abandoning his tennis whites, Clayton had shown up for this momentous occasion in a suit and tie, a bright red carnation in his lapel.

"Come in, Jaine!" Daisy said, catching sight of me. As always, she was decked out in turquoise, her Insta-Lift face beaming. "Help yourself to something to eat."

She pointed to a fine china plate laden with Ding Dongs.

"I thought we'd try something different today. Instead of petit fours, Tommy suggested we have Ding Dongs. Isn't that fun?"

I'll say this much about the guy. He may have been an appalling excuse for a human being, but I liked his taste in junk food. And yet I could not possibly allow myself to eat one of those chocolate calorie fests—not after the flourless chocolate cake I'd had for lunch.

I was still shuddering at the thought of Dickie having a smaller waist than me. I absolutely, positively had to cut down on my calories.

"Don't mind if I do," I said, reaching for one.

What can I say? I'm impossible.

Tommy grabbed one, too—instantly getting a glob of cream filling on his linen shirt—a stain certain to drive Solange bonkers.

Esme and Clayton didn't touch the Ding Dongs, however, eyeing them as if they were chocolate-covered vermin.

"Thank you so much, my dear friends," Daisy said, "for stopping by today. As you know, Jaine and I have been working on my romance, *Fifty Shades of Turquoise*, and I've asked you here to read you the first chapter."

"It's our pleasure, Daisy!" Clayton said, shooting her a worshipful smile.

Daisy cleared her throat and began reading Chapter One of our tale of love in the turquoise mines, her face flushed with pleasure at every breathless beat of Clarissa Weatherly's adventures.

The minute Daisy finished, Clayton jumped up, applauding: "Bravo! Bravo!"

Tommy, with a wink at me, chimed in: "Great job!"

Only Esme refrained from joining the chorus of praise, staring off into space, distracted. Clearly she hadn't heard a word of our purple-prosed saga.

"And what did you think, Esme?" Daisy asked, eager for approval.

"It was divine, darling," Esme replied, rousing herself from her stupor and managing a weak smile.

"Bound to be a best seller!" Clayton enthused.

"You're too kind," Daisy said, blushing.

I'll say he was. The closest that book was going to get to the best seller list would be if it were lying on top of *The New York Times Book Review*.

"And now," Clayton said, "if you don't mind, I've got something romantic I'd like to recite."

Daisy blinked in surprise.

"Why, of course, Clayton. Go right ahead."

And with that, he got down on one knee in front of Daisy.

"Daisy, my dear. From the very first day I saw you at my mailbox, I've adored you. Will you do me the very great honor of becoming my bride?"

Taking a ring box from his pocket, he opened it to reveal a mega-carat diamond engagement ring.

No wonder he was spiffed up in his suit and carnation. He'd come to propose.

Daisy flushed, taken aback.

"I'm so very sorry, Clayton. I can't marry you. I was just about to break the happy news. Tommy's asked me to marry him, and I've said yes."

Clamping a possessive arm around Daisy's shoulder, Tommy lobbed Clayton a look of sheer triumph.

Clayton and Esme just sat there, aghast.

I myself was so gobsmacked, I could hardly finish my second Ding Dong.

Chapter 13

A nd that was only Act One of the day's drama.
We were all sitting there after the wedding announcement—Daisy beaming, Tommy smirking, the rest
of us looking like mourners at a wake—when the silence
was shattered by a loud banging at the front door.

Solange hurried off to get it, and seconds later a stat-
uesque brunette with battleship boobs and legs that wouldn't
quit came charging into the room. Standing with her hands
on her hips, breathing fire, she reminded me of a low-rent
Wonder Woman.

"You no good SOB!" she cried, spotting Tommy.
"Running out on me without even a text!"

For the first time since he sauntered into La Belle Vie,
Tommy seemed rattled.

"I've been trying to track you down for ages," Wonder

Woman said through gritted teeth. "I finally found out where you were when I opened my Uber account and saw you used it to get a ride over here!"

Eyes blazing, she charged at him, straddling him as he sat on the sofa, her hands closing tight around his neck.

We all watched as Tommy struggled to pry himself free from her grip—Daisy, horrified; the rest of us loving every minute of it. I'm certain that, had we been polled, the general consensus in the room would have been, "Go, Wonder Woman!"

Alas, Tommy managed to break free.

"What's this all about, Tommy?" Daisy asked. "How do you know this young woman?"

"I'll tell you how he knows me!" Wonder Woman piped up. "He's my cheating, dirtbag of a boyfriend, and he owes me ten grand in back rent."

Oh, happy day! It looked like our collective prayers had been answered. Tommy had a jilted ex-girlfriend, whom he apparently abandoned without a smidgeon of remorse. Surely Daisy would see him for the bum that he was.

Daisy turned to Tommy, her brow wrinkled in consternation.

"Is this true?"

By now Tommy had recovered his cool.

"Yes, Daisy," he replied, smooth as silk, "it's true that Arlene and I were involved, but it was a troubled relationship from the beginning. When I met you, I'd already decided to move out. It was only when I got to know you that I discovered true love."

Oh, glug. If he spewed any more sap, he'd turn into a maple tree.

Wonder Woman's eyes grew wide with disbelief.

"You're in love with *her*?" she asked, pointing to Daisy. "But she's old!"

A harsh assessment, but sadly true.

Poor Daisy looked stricken.

Tommy put a comforting arm around her shoulder, drawing her close to his side.

"Age is just a number, Arlene. And in my eyes, Daisy is Number One."

He gazed down at Daisy, doing a great impersonation of a guy deeply in love.

And much to my dismay, Daisy seemed to melt at his touch.

"Oh, please!" Wonder Woman snorted. "I hope you're not buying any of this, lady," she said to Daisy. "Tommy's full of crap, always has been."

"Don't tell me you actually believe him?" Clayton echoed.

"Yes, Clayton," Daisy said firmly. "I do."

I felt the Ding Dongs churning in my stomach as she shot Tommy her sweet smile.

"How much does he owe you?" she asked, turning to Wonder Woman.

"Ten thousand dollars. Plus $13.75 for the Uber ride."

"I can pay you five thousand," Tommy offered. "That's how much I've saved since I started working for Daisy."

"No, Tommy," Daisy protested. "I don't want you to wipe out your savings. Wait here," she said to Wonder Woman. "I'll go write you a check. Whom shall I make it out to?"

"Arlene Zimmer."

And off Daisy went to write Arlene Zimmer a check.

Any hopes we'd entertained that Tommy would be booted out of La Belle Vie had been shattered to oblivion. It looked like Tommy had survived Wonder Woman's coup and was back on the throne, the undisputed king of the castle.

Chapter 14

And so began Tommy's reign of terror.

When I showed up for work the next morning, I found Kate huddled in the kitchen with Raymond and Solange, wallowing in misery.

Kate was eating ice cream straight from the carton while Raymond and Solange had opted for something stronger, swigging shots from a bottle of scotch.

"Daisy was just here," Kate said, scooping up a mound of fudge ripple. "She's cutting our salaries by twenty percent."

So Esme wasn't the only one who'd taken a financial hit now that Tommy was ruling the roost.

"Tommy sold Daisy some bill of goods about how she's living beyond her means and has to cut back on expenses," Solange said, taking a healthy slug of scotch.

"This from the guy who just ordered himself a Bentley." Kate rolled her eyes in disgust. "I saw the payment when I was going through Daisy's online bank account."

Raymond bypassed his shot glass and swigged straight from the bottle.

"There's no way I can work for that jerk," he said. "We have to start looking for another job, Solange."

"And risk losing the one hundred thousand Daisy's leaving us in her will?"

"Dammit, you're right. I hadn't thought of that."

I remembered Kate telling me that Daisy had left her employees money in her will, but I had no idea she'd been so generous.

It would be hard indeed to walk away from such a large inheritance.

"Looks like we're trapped working for Tommy the Terrible," Kate moaned. "Could things be any worse?"

As it turned out, they could.

That afternoon, I was banging away at *Fifty Shades* when Solange showed up and told me Daisy wanted to see me in the living room.

"She's with her attorney," Solange whispered, eyes wide with concern.

I found Daisy perched on the living room sofa, paperwork scattered in front of her on the coffee table.

Tommy, as usual, sat glued to her side.

Seated on her other side was a no-nonsense African American woman in an impeccably tailored suit.

"Jaine, dear," Daisy said. "I'd like to meet my attorney, Sandra Kass."

The attorney nodded at me briskly.

"I've made a few changes to my will," Daisy explained, "and I need you to be a witness."

"You sure you're okay with these changes?" the attorney asked, staring intently at Daisy.

"She's sure," Tommy snapped.

"Yes, of course." Daisy took Tommy's hand in hers and gave it a squeeze. "I'm absolutely sure."

"Well, then. Let's do it," said the attorney.

She handed Daisy a pen, and Daisy signed the document with a flourish. Then the attorney, acting as a witness, added her own signature.

Finally it was my turn.

"Sign right here," Sandra Kass, Esquire, said to me, "and fill in your address."

With heavy heart, I signed the document, certain that Tommy had just become a very lucky beneficiary.

"That does it," said the attorney when I'd finished. "You're all set, Daisy."

Tommy preened much like Prozac when she's just snagged an especially juicy piece of pepperoni from my pizza.

"Jaine, dear," Daisy said, handing me the will, "give this to Kate and have her file it away. And thank you so much for helping out."

"No problem," I said, making my exit.

Because Daisy's will was a private document and absolutely none of my business, I promptly proceeded to read it the minute I cleared the foyer.

My eyes bugged out at the very first paragraph.

I'd expected Tommy to inherit a nice chunk of change. But according to that momentous first paragraph, Daisy was leaving all—I repeat all—her money to Tommy. With special instructions for Tommy to take care of Solange, Raymond, and Kate in the event of her death.

Yeah, right. The only person Tommy was going to take care of was himself.

The three ex-beneficiaries, and Voodoo Tommy, were waiting for me when I got back to the office.

They cringed when I showed them the will.

"That seals it," Kate sighed. "We're screwed."

"Time to start looking for another job," Solange agreed.

"If only this thing worked," Raymond said, grabbing Voodoo Tommy from Kate's desk and giving it a particularly vicious stab in the neck.

A gesture I would remember only too well in the days to come.

Chapter 15

The lovebirds wanted a simple wedding. Just a handful of guests, with a ceremony in the living room, followed by lunch out on the patio.

Tommy had invited no one, which was no surprise to me.

All his pals were probably doing time in San Quentin.

Daisy was on cloud nine in the days leading up to the big event, lost in the throes of her May–December romance.

Sadly, she was flying solo.

Raymond, Solange, and Kate were moping around like zombies on Valium.

Clayton, usually a fixture at lunch, was nowhere to be seen. And Esme, when she dropped by to visit, was a shell of her former socialite self.

The day before the wedding, I came to work and found Esme in the living room, worry lines etched in her brow, texting on her cell phone. There was a slightly frantic air about her, as if she were sending out SOS messages from a desert island.

Once again, I remembered how stricken she'd been when Tommy threatened to slash funds to her charity.

"Hello, Jaine," she said, catching sight of me.

Why, I wondered, was she sitting there all alone?

"Hi, Esme," I replied. "Does Daisy know you're here?"

"Yes, she knows. I'm waiting for her to get dressed. Today's our spa day, her last as a single gal."

She aimed for a tone of gay insouciance but didn't even come close. Before Tommy, she'd have been upstairs with Daisy, keeping her company as she got dressed, laughing and trading tidbits of gossip.

As I bid her good-bye and stepped into the foyer, the doorbell rang.

I opened the door to find a burly, middle-aged guy in slacks and a collared polo, muscles bulging from the sleeves of his shirt.

In his hands he carried a beautifully wrapped gift box.

"Can I help you?" I asked.

"I'm Marco," he said in a gravelly voice. "Clayton Manning's valet. Mr. Manning is out of town visiting his son in Carmel, and he asked me to drop off this wedding gift."

"How nice!" I said, taking the elaborately wrapped present.

I just hoped that whatever was inside wasn't ticking.

"Would you mind if I used your restroom before I

left?" he asked. "Mr. Manning's having some plumbing work done, and they shut off the water."

"Of course."

After dropping Clayton's wedding gift on a table in the foyer, I led him to the bathroom across the hall from our office.

"Thanks," he said at the bathroom door. "I'll let myself out."

I nodded good-bye and headed into the office, where Kate was on the phone, going over last-minute instructions with the florist.

"That's right. White roses and peonies for the bridal bouquet, fresh as possible. And we need it here by eleven AM. . . . Great, thanks."

She hung up with a sigh.

"Daisy's getting the wrong flowers. She should've ordered lilies. Marrying Tommy will be like going to her own funeral."

"Where is Tommy the Terrible, anyway?" I asked.

"Who knows? Probably trolling the escort services, looking for a date to bring to his wedding."

We would have eagerly gone on trashing Tommy, but Kate's phone rang just then and she was soon caught up finalizing the newlyweds' honeymoon itinerary: Two weeks in Bali.

"How romantic!" Daisy had gushed at lunch the other day when she told us about their plans. "Tommy really needs a break!"

From what? Leafing through the Tiffany catalog?

Like Kate, I simply could not believe Daisy was foolish enough to marry this brazen nogoodnik. But there was nothing I could do about it, so I settled down at my desk to do battle with Clarissa Weatherly.

Before I could even open the *Fifty Shades* file, Tommy came bursting into the office, holding one of the tomes I'd seen in the library, a leather-bound copy of *Oliver Twist*.

"I always knew you were a lousy personal assistant," he cried, storming over to Kate. "But now I know you're a thief!"

He sprang open the copy of *Oliver Twist*, revealing—not a copy of the tale of a London street urchin—but a hollowed out box, one of those phony books people use to hide cash and valuables.

"There was two hundred dollars in here yesterday," he said, glaring at Kate. "Now it's gone. Of all the staff, you're the only one who knows about Daisy's secret hiding places. So you had to be the one who stole it."

Kate's jaw dropped in disbelief.

"Don't be crazy. I didn't take any money."

Then her eyes narrowed into suspicious slits.

"If you ask me, it was probably you. You've been robbing Daisy blind ever since you moved in."

At which point, Daisy came bustling in to join us, still in her bathrobe.

"Good heavens! What's going on in here?"

"Kate stole two hundred dollars from *Oliver Twist*," Tommy said, holding out the hollowed book.

"I did not!" Kate fumed.

"She's been taking advantage of you, Daisy," Tommy said, doing his best impression of someone who actually cared about Daisy's welfare.

"I'm not the one taking advantage of you, Daisy!"

Kate cried. "Don't you see that Tommy's nothing but a gold digger? You can't really believe he loves you. He's going to take you for everything you're worth. Get out while you still can."

Daisy's cherubic face turned stony.

"Pack your things, Kate. You're fired."

Kate gasped in disbelief. "You can't mean that."

"Indeed, I do. No one talks that way about my Tommy. I want you out of here by the time I get back from the spa."

With that, she marched out of the office, arm in arm with her boy toy.

Kate raced out into the hallway after them, me hot on her heels.

"I'm going to get you for this, Tommy!" Kate shrieked. "Big time!"

By now, Esme and Solange had joined us in the hallway, come to see what the ruckus was all about.

"Daisy, dear. Is everything okay?" Esme asked, an eager glimmer in her eyes, undoubtedly hoping that the raised voices she'd heard had been a spat between Daisy and Tommy.

"Everything's fine," Daisy assured her. "I'll be right down as soon as I finish dressing."

Daisy started for the staircase, turning back to throw Tommy a kiss.

"Don't stay too long in the tanning bed, darling. We'll be getting more than enough sun in Bali."

"I'll keep it short," he promised.

And off he sauntered to the gym, another victory under his belt.

* * *

"A fat lot of good you were!" Kate said to Voodoo Tommy, tossing him into the wastepaper basket.

Kate was busy clearing her desk, stowing her belongings in a carton she'd retrieved from the garage.

"That miserable sonofabitch framed me," she fumed. "I'd never dream of stealing from Daisy." Then she looked up at me, concerned. "You believe me, don't you?"

"Of course I do."

"Tommy probably took that cash and blamed me before Daisy could discover it was missing."

My sentiments exactly.

"I can't let Daisy fire you," I said. "I'm going to tell her about Tommy making a pass at me. She needs to know the truth."

"You'd do that for me?" Kate asked, her eyes welling with tears.

"Absolutely."

"You might want to think twice about it. If she fired me, she'll probably fire you, too. Tommy's got her totally under his spell."

She was right, of course. The minute I told Daisy about Tommy making a pass at me, I'd be right behind Kate walking out the door.

But I wouldn't be able to live with myself if I let Daisy go ahead with the wedding without speaking up. Just as I was gathering my courage to go through with my plan, a bone-chilling scream pierced the air.

I raced out into the hall and saw Daisy standing in the doorway of the gym, her body wracked with sobs.

"What's wrong?" I cried, hurrying to her side.

Tears streaming down her cheeks, she pointed inside the gym.

There was Tommy lying in his tanning bed, clad only in a pair of leopard-print thongs, goggles over his eyes, a tasteless snake tattoo on his upper thigh. And—the reason for Daisy's sobs—the sharp blade of his Swiss Army Knife plunged deep into his neck.

Time to cancel those wedding bells.

Chapter 16

"**O**h, Lord!" Daisy moaned. "I can't bear to look at him."

She pulled the door to the gym shut just as Esme came swooping down the hallway, followed by a wide-eyed Solange.

"Daisy, darling!" Esme cried. "What on earth is going on?"

"Tommy's dead," Daisy said between sobs.

"Someone stabbed him in the neck with his Swiss Army Knife," I pointed out, for anyone interested in the gory details.

Solange opened the door a crack and peeked inside, gasping at the sight of her former boss.

"Wow," she said, pulling the door shut again. "I just ironed those thongs yesterday."

Esme, who had no interest in looking at Tommy's

corpse, managed to work up a few tsks for the occasion. But I could see her heart wasn't in it.

"There, there." She clutched Daisy to her flat chest. "Everything's going to be all right."

"Oh, Esme!" Daisy cried, eyes red-rimmed with tears. "Thank heavens you're here. I don't know what I'd do without you."

Whaddya know? It looked like Esme was back in the saddle, once again Daisy's BFF. And in spite of her clucks of pity, something told me she couldn't have been happier to be rid of Tommy.

By now, I'd called 911 and soon the place was swarming with police, who ordered us to remain at La Belle Vie until we'd been questioned.

The detective on the case, Lieutenant Al Buono, was a squat guy with a military buzz cut, his lips apparently incapable of smiling. After setting up headquarters in the dining room, he summoned Daisy for questioning.

"I'll go with you, hon," Esme offered, "for moral support."

"Afraid not," said one of the detective's underlings, a string bean of a man who, for the purposes of this story, shall be known as Barney Fife. "Detective Buono needs to speak with Ms. Kincaid alone."

Once Daisy was led away, Esme returned to the living room while Solange sought refuge in her bedroom.

Raymond, I noticed, was nowhere to be seen.

Kate and I waited our turn to be questioned in our office, fortified by a carton of fudge ripple sprinkled with M&M's.

(Oh, don't go shaking your head. Like you've never thought of trying it.)

Kate was spooning the stuff into her mouth, near frantic with fear.

"It can't look good," she said between swallows. "My having that big fight with Tommy right before he got killed."

"Try not to worry, hon. Everybody hated the guy. The police will have suspects up their ying-yang."

"But I'm the only one who threated to get him—big time. I'm no homicide expert, but I can see how that might be construed as a death threat."

She had a point. I have to confess that if I were in her shoes, I'd be a tad hysterical. A feeling that was reinforced when Barney Fife showed up at our office to summon Kate to the hot seat.

"Hold on a sec," Barney said as Kate got up to join him. "What's this?"

He pointed to Voodoo Tommy in the trash can, studded with straight pins.

"Um . . . er . . . a doll?" Kate replied, beads of sweat popping on her brow.

Whipping on a pair of rubber gloves, the cop removed Voodoo Tommy from the trash.

"It's got pins all over it. And the victim's name on its chest. What is this thing, anyway? A voodoo doll?"

"Kinda sorta," Kate admitted.

"And who does it belong to?"

"That would be me," Kate squeaked, her voice oozing panic.

"Is that so?" he said, with a withering look.

Yikes. I could practically hear a jail cell door clanging shut behind her.

"Follow me," Barney said, after plopping the doll into a plastic bag.

And Kate set off behind him, Dead Chocoholic Walking.

Fifteen minutes later, a stricken Kate came staggering back to the office, convinced she was going to be arrested for Tommy's murder. Not only had the cops found Voodoo Tommy, but apparently Esme claimed she saw Kate going into the gym around the time of the murder.

"Did you?" I asked, jolted by this latest newsflash.

"Yes," Kate confessed. "After I picked up my moving carton from the garage, I was still so furious with Tommy, I marched over to the gym and told him to go to hell. But he was alive when I got there. I swear I didn't kill him."

And I believed her.

I mean, nobody who eats M&M's with fudge ripple could possibly be a killer.

That's my scientific opinion, anyway.

YOU'VE GOT MAIL!

To: Jausten
From: Shoptillyoudrop
Subject: Rodin Reincarnated

If I thought Daddy's new haircut was impossible to live with, things are even worse now that he's discovered sculpting. Ever since we started our class, Daddy's convinced he's Rodin reincarnated, certain he's going to take the art world by storm.

He's become positively insufferable, running around Tampa Vistas, collaring anyone who can stand the stink of his hair, yakking about the joys of sculpting, tossing out words like "armature" and "vitrification"—which I'm sure he filched from an online sculpting glossary.

Meanwhile, his Statue of Liberty is a lumpy mess.

XOXO,
Mom

To: Jausten
From: DaddyO
Subject: Natural Born Sculptor

Dearest Lambchop—I'm proud to report I'm making great progress on my Statue of Liberty. What an amazing likeness it bears to the real thing.

I guess I'm just a natural-born sculptor. The clay seems to spring to life at the touch of my fingers. Truly magical to behold!

And to think I almost didn't take the class. What a loss that would have been to the art world.

Love 'n cuddles from,
DaddyO

To: Jausten
From: Shoptillyoudrop
Subject: Dead on the Spot!

Oh, my goodness! You'll never guess what just happened! Daddy and I were out on the patio having lunch when a housefly started buzzing around Daddy's hair. Daddy tried to swat it away, but he needn't have bothered. The poor critter took one whiff of Big Al's Hair Wax and dropped dead on the spot!

I tell you, your father is a menace to all creatures great and small!

XOXO,
Mom

To: Jausten
From: Shoptillyoudrop
Subject: I Finally Did It!

I finally did it, sweetheart! After seeing that poor house-fly plummet to his death, I screwed up my courage and threw away Big Al's Hair Wax in Edna Lindstrom's garbage can. Then I washed out the jar and filled it with another styling wax I bought at CVS.

Daddy will probably never know the difference, as he can't seem to smell anything these days.

XOXO,
Mom

To: Jausten
From: DaddyO
Subject: Perfidy!

You're not going to believe this, Lambchop, but your sweet, sainted mother actually threw away Big Al's Hair Wax and tried to pawn off an inferior substitute.

But she couldn't fool me. After several hours searching, I finally found Big Al's magical elixir in a baggie in Edna Lindstrom's trash, where your mom had diabolically tossed it.

I'm still stung by her betrayal.

Your grievously wounded,
DaddyO

To: Jausten
From: Shoptillyoudrop
Subject: Darn it All!

Daddy found Big Al's Hair Wax in Edna's garbage.
Darn it all. I knew I should have brought it to a
hazardous waste dump.

XOXO,
Mom

Chapter 17

The next morning I was on the sofa, scarfing down a cinnamon raisin bagel and reading about Tommy's murder in the *Los Angeles Times*—in an article headlined SLEAZY GIGOLO FOUND DEAD IN TANNING BED.

Okay, so it was MAN FOUND DEAD IN TANNING BED.

Daisy's attorney was quoted as saying, "Ms. Kincaid is bereft at the loss of her beloved fiancé."

"Everyone else is pleased as punch!" were the words she did not add.

Prozac sat curled up across from me on my armchair, belching minced mackerel fumes and studiously ignoring me.

I'd been spending quite a bit of time at Dickie's condo, which irked her no end. It was no use telling her that

Dickie and I would happily spend more time at my place if only she hadn't turned my apartment into a war zone.

"Come here, sweetpea," I cajoled, "and let me rub you behind your ears."

She graced me with her most withering stink eye.

Not in the mood. Go scratch Dickie's ears.

With a sigh, I returned to the story of Tommy's murder, relieved to see there was no mention of Kate as the cops' prime suspect.

But I feared that's what she was.

Soon after Kate had returned from her interview, I was summoned for a little chat with Lieutenant Buono. He sat at the head of the dining room table, ramrod stiff, his lips a thin grim line.

When asked about Voodoo Tommy, I tried to assure the dour detective that it was all just a joke, that Kate never expressed any desire to kill Tommy.

"Except," he noted, "when she threatened to get him 'big time.'"

"I'm sure she didn't mean it," I offered lamely.

"Any idea who else might have wanted him dead?" he asked.

"It's a long list."

I did not go into specifics, unwilling to throw anyone under the bus. The cops would dig up all the facts soon enough. But my head was swimming with suspects. Tommy had aced the household staff out of their inheritances and pushed Clayton and Esme out of Daisy's life.

"So many people hated Tommy," I said.

"But only one of them, according to the testimony of Esme Larkin, was seen heading to the gym at the time of the murder," Lieutenant Buono pointed out. "Your friend Kate."

Darn that blabbermouth Esme.

After a few more perfunctory questions, the dour detective set me free, and I headed back to the office, convinced that Kate was his prime suspect.

As it turned out that next morning, I was right.

Just as I was polishing off my cinnamon raisin bagel, I got a call from Kate. If anything, she was even more frantic than she'd been yesterday.

"Last night the police brought me in for more questioning. They kept me there for hours, asking me the same questions over and over again. Finally, when I asked for an attorney, they got me a court-appointed dufus who doesn't know a tort from a tortilla. I just know I'm going to be arrested!" she wailed.

"Hang in there, honey. Let me see what I can do to help."

"How can you help?" she asked.

I filled her in on my adventures as a part-time, semi-professional PI, stirring sagas you can read about in the titles at the front of this book.

"You?" she asked. "A private eye???"

I get that reaction a lot.

When I assured her that I had indeed solved my fair share of murders, she was giddy with relief.

"I just know you're going to get me out of this mess!"

She hung up in a flurry of 'thank yous,' and I wondered if maybe I'd oversold myself just a tad.

Now I really had to get her off the hook.

The pressure was on.

I was fortifying myself with another CRB and reading about Mom's foiled attempt to get rid of Big Al's Hair Wax when Lance came knocking at my door.

Like Prozac, he was ticked off about all the time I'd been spending with Dickie.

"Hello, Jaine," he said, more than a hint of frost in his voice. "Long time, no see."

From her perch on the armchair, Prozac gave a commiserating meow.

Tell me about it. I'm surprised she still remembers our names.

"Poor Prozac," Lance cooed, scooping her up in his arms. "Has Jaine been ignoring you, too? Well, don't you worry. Uncle Lance still loves you."

He then proceeded to plaster her with a nauseating bunch of baby kisses.

Talk about chewing the scenery.

"So what's new with The Blob?" Lance asked when he'd finally stopped slobbering over Pro.

"I wish you'd stop calling him that."

"Why not? That's what you always used to call him."

"How many times do I have to tell you? Dickie's changed!"

"I saw the picture you posted on Instagram. The one with you and Dickie drinking lemongrass smoothies."

It's true. I'd actually glugged down one of those disgusting concoctions to score points with my adorable ex.

"Whenever I offer you one of my smoothies," Lance huffed, "you practically bite my head off."

Once again, he spoke the truth. Lance has forever been trying to get me to eat his ghastly health foods, efforts I've fought with every fiber of my elastic waist pants.

"So?" I shrugged. "I've seen the error of my ways."

"Really?" he asked, eyeing my CRB slathered with butter and strawberry jam.

"Okay, okay. I don't eat healthy when Dickie's not around. But I'm sure I'll get the hang of it eventually."

"To be perfectly honest, Jaine, I'm very hurt."

He settled down with Prozac in his lap, scratching the very ears I'd offered to scratch just a little while ago.

"Now that you've got a guy in your life, you have no time for me. I thought we were friends. Friends don't desert friends when they find a new boyfriend."

Was he kidding? I can't tell you how many times Lance has gone AWOL with a new hottie, leaving me alone with only Ben and Jerry for company.

But just because he did it to me didn't make it right.

"I'm sorry, Lance. I'm afraid I have been neglecting you. Let's get together one night, the three of us."

"Dickie, too?" Lance said, not bothering to hide his disappointment.

"I'm sure once you get to know him, you'll like him."

"Well, okay," Lance agreed. "I'll do it. I've missed you terribly, honey."

In his lap, Prozac purred.

I've missed you, too, sweetums.

Chapter 18

I showed up at La Belle Vie later that morning, wondering if I still had a job.

Now that Tommy was dead, I feared Daisy would lose interest in her steamy romance novel and cut me free. I was actually growing fond of C. Weatherly, that passionate turquoise miner, and would be sad to see her bite the dust.

Not only that, I'd checked my contract and discovered that if for any reason I didn't finish the book, Daisy would not be paying me ten grand, but a vastly reduced $2,500.

After stowing my purse in the office, which seemed awfully lonely without Kate (and Voodoo Tommy), I wandered over to the gym.

The police had finished their crime scene investigation, and the only memento of the murder was a rusted blood stain on the tanning bed where Tommy's head had been.

I stared at the tanning bed, remembering Tommy's lifeless body in his god-awful leopard print thong, the ugly snake tattoo on his upper thigh, his beloved Swiss Army Knife plunged into his neck.

What a grisly way to go.

Trying to erase that gruesome image from my mind, I made my way to the kitchen for a cup of coffee. There I found Solange and Raymond knocking back mimosas and croissants.

"Wonderful news!" Solange exclaimed when she saw me. "Raymond and I just spoke with Daisy, and she's raising our salaries back to where they were before Tommy cut them."

"She said she realized how much she needed us and couldn't afford to lose us," Raymond grinned.

"Just think!" Solange clinked her mimosa glass against Raymond's. "I'll never have to iron one of Tommy's stupid thongs again!"

"Bye-bye, Tater Tots!" Raymond added, returning her clink.

Something told me they'd be back in Daisy's will, too.

"Mimosa, Jaine?" Raymond asked.

"Thanks, but it's a bit too early for me."

I left them slugging down their mimosas and headed back to the office, where I settled down at my desk with my coffee (and the weensiest sliver of croissant).

I'd just opened *Fifty Shades* and was about to reunite with C. Weatherly when Daisy wandered in, wearing wrinkled pajamas and terry robe. Her pixie cut lay flat and greasy against her scalp; her face haggard and etched with wrinkles.

No Insta-Lift for Daisy that day.

In her hands she held a teacup, the contents of which smelled an awful lot like bourbon.

"Jaine, dear," she said, taking a slug of her "tea." "We need to talk."

Oh, hell. I could practically see my ten grand sprouting wings and flying out the window.

"Would you mind awfully taking over Kate's duties until I can find a suitable replacement?"

Yay! She hadn't cut me off from the book after all!

"It won't involve much work," she promised. "I don't plan on making very many social engagements in the foreseeable future."

That said with a small, sad smile.

"I don't mind at all," I assured her.

"Wonderful." She started for the door, then stopped. "I almost forgot. The book."

Dammit. Here's where I got the ax.

"How's it coming along?"

"Fine," I said. "Do you still want me to work on it?"

"Yes, of course. Why wouldn't I?"

"I thought maybe, what with Tommy's death, you might have soured on the project."

"No, I can't let that stop me. I'll admit I'm not terribly enthused about *Fifty Shades of Turquoise* at the moment, but I refuse to abandon it."

Her spine stiffened with resolve.

"I threw away my life once, and I'm not about to do it again. Don't misunderstand," she added. "I'll always treasure my days with Tommy. The only other man who ever made me feel so special was my father."

She reached over and picked up the framed photo of

herself as a toddler on her father's lap and gazed at it wistfully.

"What about Clayton?" I asked. "He seems crazy about you."

"Clayton is a darling man, and I'm very fond of him, but I'll never feel the same way about him as I did about Tommy."

She stared out into space, eyes misted with tears, perhaps envisioning Tommy lying by the pool, working on his tan.

"It may take a while," she said, "but I'm determined to get through this. So keep writing, Jaine."

With that, she drifted out of the room, the distinct scent of bourbon in her wake.

Chapter 19

Daisy spent the day in bed in her pajamas, watching movies on TCM, Esme glued to her side. The Bel Air charity doyenne had come whooshing in on a cloud of designer perfume, bearing lilies in one hand and a vat of chicken soup in the other—clearly thrilled to resume her former role as Daisy's BFF.

Everybody wanted Tommy dead, but something told me Esme wanted it most of all.

I thought about how eager she'd been to throw Kate under the bus, blabbing to the police about how she'd seen Kate heading to the gym before the murder.

And I remembered the look of sheer panic on her face when Tommy threatened to slash Daisy's contributions to her charity.

Now I wondered: Why had Esme been so shattered by Tommy's threat? True, a cut from a major donor would be upsetting but not devastating. Surely she had other donors willing to back her efforts to coddle the homeless fur-babies of Bel Air.

My suspicions aroused, I Googled the Bel Air Animal Welfare League.

The website came up on the screen—a single home page with a blurry photo of Esme holding a puppy.

Aside from that, there was nothing. Zippo. Zero board members. No kennels. And most important, no charity registration number.

Could it be? Was Esme running a scam?

I needed to speak to her alone, without Daisy.

Checking Kate's computer, I found Esme's address in Daisy's contacts file and drove over there the next morning before work.

Much to my surprise, I discovered that the Bel Air society matron did not live in Bel Air. Nowhere close. Instead I found her in that no man's land between Westwood and Santa Monica known as West Los Angeles.

Her house was one of those architectural orphans, a squat single-family home hemmed in on both sides by looming apartment buildings, a holdover from earlier years when the street was completely residential.

After snagging a parking spot, I made my way up the front path to Esme's house, past a patch of lawn that hadn't seen a sprinkler system in decades, bordered by azaleas thick with dust.

I tried to peek inside, but all the windows were shrouded in heavy drapes.

The place was so rundown, for a minute I wondered if I was at the wrong address.

I rang a rusty doorbell, and seconds later the door swung open.

Esme stood there, tall and stately in a floral silk kimono, out of place amidst her modest surroundings.

A look of shock flitted across her face; then she quickly regained her composure.

"How nice to see you, Jaine!" she lied.

In her hand, I noticed, she held a most yummy looking chocolate glazed donut.

"Do you mind if I come in for a minute?" I asked.

"Not at all," she fibbed again, ushering me into a tiny living room decorated with furniture that can only be described as Early Econo-Lodge.

"Excuse the decor. I'm staying here in my maid's house while I have my Bel Air estate tented for termites."

"That's strange," I said. "This is the only address Daisy has for you in her files."

She smiled stiffly, and I could practically see the wheels spinning in her brain as she decided whether to try foisting another lie on me.

I guess she figured it was hopeless.

"Okay, you got me," she said, sinking down onto a worn chenille sofa. "This is my humble abode."

Accent on the humble.

"Do me a favor, will you? I've never had Daisy over here, and I'd appreciate it if you wouldn't tell her the truth about where I live."

"Fine," I said. "Your secret's safe with me. This one, anyway."

She gazed at me warily. "What do you mean?"

"I checked out the website for the Bel Air Animal Welfare League," I said, sitting on a frayed armchair. "It

doesn't look like much of a site. Or a charity, for that matter. Have you been lying to Daisy about that, too?"

"Got me again," she groaned, listlessly tossing her donut onto a rickety TV tray.

"The charity's not a complete fake, though. I do make donations to the local ASPCA. But I use most of the money to pay my expenses. The rent on this hellhole is astronomical, and I've got to dress the part if I want to keep up my image."

"I see," I nodded, barely restraining myself from grabbing her abandoned donut. That chocolate glaze looked scrumptious.

"I used to have real money," Esme was saying, "back when my husband was alive. But then he upped and died on me, and things went downhill fast.

"Things got so bad I had to take a job as a saleslady at Saks. That's where I met Daisy. I was on my lunch break at Saks's restaurant. Daisy came and sat next to me, and the next thing I knew we'd struck up a conversation. She just assumed from my designer clothes that I was a customer, not an employee. And I didn't have the courage to tell her the truth.

"The more I got to know her, the more I realized what a generous soul she was. And she had so much money, I figured she wouldn't miss a couple of grand a month to keep me afloat. So I started the Bel Air Animal Welfare League. Daisy bought into it completely and started writing me very generous checks.

"It was all going great until Tommy came along and convinced Daisy to cut my funding."

She grimaced in disgust.

"What an odious young man. Picking his teeth at th

table, cleaning the gunk from under his nails, and that dreadful tattoo of a snake on his thigh. Ugh. A total thug. I can't believe Daisy was foolish enough to fall for him."

She retrieved her abandoned donut and took a half-hearted bite.

(How anyone can be halfhearted when eating a chocolate glazed donut is beyond me.)

"What's with all these questions, anyway?" Esme asked, suddenly suspicious. "Last I heard, you were a writer, not a police officer."

"I'm trying to help Kate clear her name. Apparently, she's the prime suspect in the case."

"As well she should be. I saw her heading toward the gym right before the murder. And she'd practically threatened to kill Tommy. Everybody heard her screaming at him. It all points to her being the killer, don't you think?"

"Not necessarily. It could easily have been someone else."

She saw where this train of thought was chugging.

"Surely you can't suspect me!"

"Maybe just a tad," I admitted. "After all, Tommy was cutting off your financial lifeline."

At that she sat up straight, starch returning to her spine.

"Tommy was a dreadful man, and I absolutely loathed him. But I can assure you I didn't kill him."

Fire burned her eyes, a flame of righteous indignation.

She was either telling the truth or a darn good actress.

"Well, thanks for your time," I said, getting up. "I'd better be going."

"I hope you won't be telling Daisy about my charity 'irregularities.'" Esme smiled imploringly. "It's more than

just the money. I'm really very fond of her and would be heartbroken to lose her friendship."

Once again, her words rang true.

I agreed not to say anything and headed out the door, ready to scratch her off my suspect list.

It was only when I was back in my Corolla driving over to Krispy Kreme for some chocolate-glazed donuts that I remembered what Esme said about Tommy's snake tattoo. Tommy had always worn boxer shorts at the pool; his upper thighs never visible.

And the door to the gym was closed when Esme came rushing over to join us right after the murder.

So how on earth had Esme known about Tommy's tattoo—unless she'd seen it before stabbing him to death?

Chapter 20

Daisy was waiting for me when I showed up at La Belle Vie—sitting at my desk in her pajamas, staring at the picture of her beloved billionaire daddy.

At her elbow was a steaming mug of "tea."

I could smell the bourbon from across the room.

"Jaine, dear," she said, catching sight of me. "I need you to make some arrangements."

It turned out that Tommy's next of kin, an estranged sister in Alaska, did not give a flying frisbee about her brother's remains and had happily released them to Daisy.

"I'm going to have Tommy cremated and scatter his ashes at sea. I want to do it in Malibu near the restaurant we were so fond of." She smiled at the memory of her happy lunches with Tommy the Terrible. "So I need you to charter a yacht and make all the arrangements."

"Not a problem," I assured her.

"And I'd like to see some more pages from our book when you get a chance," she added. "I've thought it over, and I've decided it will be a good distraction for me."

Thus saddled with a boatload of work, I passed the day in a flurry of phone calls and heaving bosoms, with no time to pursue my murder investigation.

At five I had to rush off and meet Dickie. I'd agreed to join him at his spin class. For once, I was actually looking forward to working out—eager to turn over a new leaf and spin my calories away.

And I had plenty that needed spinning, especially after that pit stop at Krispy Kreme.

Having scarfed down a couple of chocolate-glazed beauties, I'd decided to skip lunch. Which was all very noble, but left me starving at five PM when I hurried home to change into athletic togs.

Needless to say, I did not own a pair of bike shorts (the last thing my thighs needed were to be squished into skintight Spandex), so I threw on some old sweats.

Then I opened a can of Hearty Halibut Innards for Prozac, who'd been thumping her tail with displeasure as she watched me get dressed.

You're going out again?? Who's going to give me my after-dinner belly rub?

But her snit fit was forgotten the minute she sniffed those halibut innards, and soon she was swan diving into her chow with the expertise of an ace fighter pilot.

I, too, was quite the speed demon as I scarfed down some emergency Oreos before taking off for Dickie's gym in Santa Monica.

Sad to say, those emergency Oreos did not even begin to appease my raging appetite.

I tried to ignore my hunger pangs, but it was no use.

Which is why, as I pulled into the gym parking lot, I reached into my glove compartment for a bag of emergency M&M's.

(I'll say this about me. When it comes to junk food, I'm always prepared for an emergency.)

Just as I popped a handful in my mouth, I saw Dickie driving into the lot.

Damn! I couldn't let him see me cheating on Hapi's god-awful diet. I gulped down the M&M's as quickly as I could, shoving the rest of them into my sweatpants pocket.

By now, Dickie had spotted my Corolla and pulled up alongside me.

Frantically, I checked my smile in my rearview mirror to make sure I had no chocolate on my teeth.

"Hi, bunny face," Dickie said when I got out of my car. As he zeroed in for a quick kiss, I prayed he wouldn't smell the chocolate on my breath.

Luckily he didn't.

"C'mon," he said. "I can't wait till you try spinning. You're going to love it!"

And off I trotted, happily picturing myself frolicking on the beach in the new bikini I intended to buy just as soon as I'd spun myself into shape.

My enthusiasm quickly plummeted, however, when we walked into the class and I saw a sea of gorgeous blondes with washboard abs.

And those were just the men.

Oh, foo. I had just entered one of L.A.'s many No-Fat zones.

I almost expected alarm bells to go off, alerting everyone to my presence.

(*Cellulite in the house! Cellulite in the house!*)

"Here you go," Dickie said, leading me over to one of the bikes, a hulking machine that was a lot higher than I expected.

Somehow I managed to hoist myself astride—all in all, a most excruciating experience.

What sadist invented the bike seat anyway? That thing was so darn intrusive, it practically needed a condom.

"Okay, everybody," I heard a deep voice growling. "Let's do this."

Up at the front of the class was our instructor, a guy so buff his muscles had muscles. I'm sure in another life he was either a gladiator or a Sherman Tank.

"It's spin time!" he shouted.

And so began my stint in Spin Hell.

I struggled in vain to keep up with the others as their legs spun in a blur to the music blaring from two powerful speakers.

Yikes. It was like trekking up Mount Everest.

I huffed and puffed for what felt like hours but was in actuality only three and a half minutes. Just when I thought I could not cycle one more millimeter, our musclebound leader called out:

"Okay, let's kick it up a notch!"

Kick it up a notch? Was he insane? One more notch and I'd be at St. John's cardiac unit.

Cursing myself for ever agreeing to come to this stupid class, I glanced over at Dickie, who was staring wide-eyed at the carpet beneath my bike.

I followed his gaze and would have gasped if I'd had any breath left.

There, scattered beneath my bike, was a sea of brightly colored dots.

Gaak. My M&M's!

As I discovered when the nightmarish session finally came to an end, I had a hole in the pocket of my sweatpants that had allowed those little rascals to escape. Now Dickie and all the other washboard abbers knew the truth about me, that I was a diet scofflaw who stocked her sweatpants with M&M's.

Mortified, I got down on my knees to pick them up. Dickie knelt beside me to help.

"I'm so embarrassed," I said, afraid to look him in the eye. "I skipped lunch and was absolutely starving. And then I found these in my glove compartment."

Notice how I did not mention the chocolate-glazed donuts and Oreos I'd scarfed down before our rendezvous.

Working up my courage, I looked up and saw that Dickie was smiling his sweet-sexy smile.

"No need to be embarrassed," he said. "As Hapi has taught me, *I accept that everyone is doing the best they can with what they have.*"

I could practically see Prozac upchucking a hairball at this latest affirmation. But I loved every syllable of it.

Especially when Dickie leaned in and kissed me on the nose, right there in front of all those fab-ab hotties.

Was he the best or what?

I floated out of spin class in a happy glow. Which lasted all of about seven seconds until Dickie said, "I can't wait to do this again. Next time we'll meet at the smoothie bar for lemongrass shakes. That should give you plenty of energy."

Next time? Glug!

"Sounds great," I managed to say, already working on the knee injury I planned to fake to get out of going.

No way was I showing up at another spin class. No, siree. From then on, I'd burn off my calories the old-fashioned way—by jogging to the freezer aisle for a pint of Chunky Monkey.

Chapter 21

That night I dreamed I was trapped on a spin class bike, being chased by a mob of giant M&M's, cursing me for having scarfed down so many of their relatives.

Sweat gushed from my pores as I pedaled my heart out. But no matter how fast I pedaled, the bike refused to move. In no time, the M&M's had me surrounded and were using me as a human bull's-eye—pelting my chest with stinging darts.

It was then that I woke up and realized that the stinging in my chest was just Prozac, clawing me awake for her breakfast.

She'd been cold as ice when I came home from the spin class last night.

"Oh, Pro," I'd moaned, my privates still aching from

that torture chamber of a bike seat. "Every inch of me hurts."

She'd barely glanced up from the hairball she'd just deposited on one of my cashmere sweaters.

That's what you get for leaving me alone while you go out gallivanting with The Affirmation Kid.

Clearly I had a long way to go in my efforts to win her over to Team Dickie.

Banishing all thoughts of Prozac—and my ghastly M&M's fiasco—I showed up at La Belle Vie that morning eager to resume my investigation.

I definitely needed to chat with Raymond and Solange. Both of them had their salaries slashed under Tommy's tyrannical rule and would have lost out on a hefty inheritance had he tied the knot with Daisy.

More than enough motive for murder, don't you think?

After a morning toiling in the turquoise mines, I tracked down Solange in her room, taking her afternoon break.

"Come in," she called out after I knocked on her door.

I walked in and blinked, more than a little taken aback. The place looked like a tornado had just whizzed through it—clothes, shoes, and grooming aids scattered everywhere.

Solange was lounging on her unmade bed, sheets tangled, in pajama shorts and tourniquet-tight tank top.

Her hair, normally coiled in a French twist, was loose and tousled, her long legs bare, not a speck of flab on her thighs. She looked up from the copy of *Vogue* she was reading, a half-eaten banana at her side.

"Excuse the mess," she said, gesturing at the surrounding chaos. "What with all the cleaning I do around here, I don't have the energy to keep my own room neat."

I'll say, I thought, spotting a dust bunny the size of Prozac.

"So what's up?" she asked.

"Actually, I stopped by to talk about Tommy's murder. The police think Kate is the killer, and I'm trying to help clear her name. Okay if we have a little chat?"

"Sure," she said, patting the mattress next to her.

After clearing away the banana, two fashion magazines, and a curling iron, I joined her on her bed.

"You really think Kate is innocent?" Solange asked. "After all, Esme saw her heading for the gym right before Tommy was killed."

"She did go to the gym but only to curse Tommy out. She swears he was alive when she left."

"I guess that's possible," Solange said, plucking an emery board from the sheets.

"I don't suppose you saw anyone going to the gym?" I asked as she began filing her nails.

"No, I was busy in the dining room polishing silver for the wedding brunch. Such a dirty job. My nails were an absolute wreck afterward."

It was then that I glanced down and saw something very odd. Nestled between a comb and a jar of moisturizer were a pair of pink lace panties.

It wasn't the panties that intrigued me—I could easily picture Solange strutting her stuff in them—but rather what I saw peeking out from under them: a business card embossed with the words

Tommy LaSalle
Executive Financial Planner

It was one of the cards Daisy had printed for Tommy when he was pretending to look for work.

"How interesting," I said, lifting it out from under the panties. "May I ask what Tommy's business card is doing in your bed?"

Solange groaned at the sight of it.

"It must've fallen out of his pocket when he came to see me."

"He came to see you here? In your room?"

"He snuck in while Daisy was out having her hair done and Raymond was away at the market."

"What did he want?"

"To blackmail me into having sex with him."

"Blackmail?"

Why was I not surprised? Sounded like something right up Tommy's crooked alley.

"What sort of hold did he have on you?"

After a beat of hesitation, Solange sighed deeply and said, "I may as well come clean with you. Sooner or later I'm going to have to tell Daisy the truth, too."

"About what?"

"Remember that two hundred dollars Tommy claimed Kate stole from Daisy's hollowed-out book?"

Indeed I did. It was what precipitated Kate's angry outburst, which might one day be held against her in a court of law.

"Kate didn't take that money. I did."

She looked up from her emery board, sheepish.

"I couldn't help myself. It was so tempting. You see, Daisy has a thing about being ready in case of a disaster. You know about her panic room, right?"

"No. What panic room?"

"Right next to the office. Lots of people in Bel Air

have one. A place to hide during a home invasion. But to be extra-safe, Daisy also keeps wads of cash stashed throughout the house. I found a list of her hiding places one day while I was snooping in her lingerie drawer. And I've been siphoning off money ever since."

"But why? I thought Daisy was paying you and Raymond a very generous salary."

"Not generous enough to pay for all this."

She gestured to the sea of clothing strewn about the room, and for the first time, I realized it was pretty pricey stuff.

Picking up a blouse from the floor, I checked the label: Dolce and Gabbana.

"They're all designer labels," she said. "Top of the line. My name is Solange," she added with a wry smile, "and I'm a shopaholic. Tommy caught me stealing and threatened to report me to the police unless I slept with him. Tommy only accused Kate because he wanted an excuse to fire her."

"So did you sleep with him?"

"No, I told him I was coming down with a cold and got rid of him. But I knew sooner or later he'd be back. Thank God he died when he did."

The minute the words were out of her mouth, I could tell she regretted them.

"But I swear," she insisted, her eyes wide with what may or may not have been innocence, "I didn't kill him. You've got to believe me."

As far as I was concerned, the jury was still out on that one.

Tommy had been threatening to send our gal Solange to jail. Seemed liked a very good reason to trot over to the gym and whack him in the jugular with a Swiss Army Knife.

Chapter 22

After extracting a solemn vow from Solange to never again raid Daisy's cash reserves, I headed off to the kitchen for a *tête-à-tête* with Raymond.

I found him at the kitchen island, chopping vegetables with impressive speed.

"Hey, Raymond. What're you making?"

"*Tarte au poulet*. A French chicken pot pie. Comfort food for Daisy. It was one of my signature dishes when I was executive chef at Christophe."

"Sounds yummy!"

"I'll save you some," he said with a wink.

Someday, if I ever get really rich, I'm going to buy myself a Raymond.

I was lost in a reverie of creamy chicken and chopped veggies nestled in a flaky pastry crust when Raymond said, "Can I help you?"

Oh, right. The murder. When it comes to flaky pastry crusts, I get easily distracted.

"Just stopped by for a snack," I said, grabbing an orange from a bowl on the island, reluctant to come right out and ask this talented kitchen whiz if he'd bumped off his boss from hell. Not while he was wielding a knife, anyway.

"I can't get over Tommy's murder," I said, as casually as possible. "I know everyone hated him. But still . . ."

"If you ask me, Kate did us all a favor. I'm prepared to kick in big bucks for her defense fund."

"I don't think Kate's the killer. She swore to me she didn't do it, and I believe her."

"Well, then, who did?" he asked.

"That's what I've been trying to figure out. Did you see anything out of the ordinary the morning of the murder?"

"No," he said, with a shake of his ponytail. "I wasn't even here."

Thinking back to that morning, I realized I hadn't seen him anywhere.

"I was at Home Depot picking out a coffee table with Andre."

"Andre?"

"My brother. He does odd jobs for Daisy around the house. Carpentry. Minor plumbing repairs. He's got taste up his wazoo, and he wanted my help picking out something nice. By the time I got back, Tommy was already dead."

"Any idea who could have done it? Other than Kate?"

"Let me see," he said, putting down his knife to think it over. "Clayton was out of town, so that lets him out. I was at Home Depot. And Solange couldn't possibly have done it."

Oh, yes, she could, were the words I was tactful enough not to utter.

"Maybe it was Esme," Raymond suggested. "She sure hated Tommy. One day she came storming into the kitchen for some aspirin, muttering about what a miserable SOB he was. Maybe she was the one who took him out.

"And of course," he added with a sly smile, "there's always you."

"Me? Why would I want to kill Tommy?"

"Who knows? Maybe he was bad-mouthing your book to Daisy, trying to get her to pull the plug on the project."

Oh, Lord. I only hoped the cops weren't thinking along those lines.

"Don't get your panties in an uproar," he said, seeing the look of alarm on my face. "All I know is I'm thrilled to be rid of the blackmailing bastard."

With that, he picked up his knife and resumed eviscerating his veggies.

Whoa, Nelly. Did you hear what I heard? Raymond had just called Tommy a blackmailing bastard. How did he know Tommy was into blackmail? Had Solange told him about Tommy's trip to her bedroom? Or had Raymond come home early from the market and seen Tommy sneak into her room? Had he stood outside, listening to Tommy trying to coerce his beloved into sex?

Filled to the gills with pay cuts and Tater Tots, had Raymond reached a boiling point and gotten rid of his detested boss for good?

One thing was for sure, I thought, as I watched him hack away at those veggies.

He certainly had the knife skills for the job.

Chapter 23

I trotted back to my office with my Dove Bar—you didn't really think I picked up an orange, did you?—eager to check out Raymond's alibi.

Raymond claimed he'd been with his brother, Andre, Daisy's handyman, the morning of the murder.

But I wasn't about to take his word for it.

Scrolling down Daisy's contact list, I found Andre's address and later that afternoon set out to question him.

It took me close to an hour on the 405 freeway (where every hour is rush hour) to get to Andre's digs in Hawthorne, a working class city far from the rarefied hills of Bel Air.

Andre's place was the eyesore of the block—a postage stamp of a house with peeling paint, grassless front yard, and burglary bars on the windows.

It made Esme's cottage look like Versailles.

I knocked on the door and heard shuffling footsteps inside. Then the door swung open, revealing a scruffy thirty-something guy with greasy hair down to his I PEE IN POOLS T-shirt.

He blinked at me, glassy-eyed.

"Whaddaya want?" was his gracious greeting.

"I was wondering if I could have a few minutes of your time to talk to you about Tommy LaSalle's murder."

"Nope," he said, slamming the door in my face.

This happens to me a lot. And I was prepared. Time for Plan B.

Reaching into my purse, I pulled out my trusty USDA meat inspector's badge I'd picked up years ago at a flea market. I can't tell you how many times it's come in handy when questioning a reluctant witness. Especially one as spaced out as Andre.

Once again I knocked on his door.

"Go away!" he shouted.

Yeah, right. As if that was going to happen.

"LAPD!" I called out.

"Fooey!" I heard him say as he shuffled back to the door.

(You know by now that "fooey" wasn't the "F" word he really used, right?)

"You a cop?" he asked when he yanked open the door.

"Lieutenant Mildred Pierce," I said, paying homage to one of my all-time favorite movies.

I flashed him my badge, and he glanced at it briefly, not bothering to read the words. Most people don't.

As he waved me inside, I was hit with the overwhelming smell of marijuana. Five deep breaths and I'd be high as a kite.

I followed him past a musty foyer into an even mustier

living room, where a TV was blasting an episode of *SpongeBob SquarePants*.

"I just love that dude," Andre said, nodding at the animated sponge.

Of course he did. The two shared the same IQ.

Looking around, I saw the room was furnished with pieces straight from the Abandoned in an Alley collection—pea green and yellow plaid sofa and matching armchair, both covered with a colorful assortment of stains.

But all that I was interested in was Andre's coffee table. And there it was, right in front of the sofa: a battered piece of wood etched with cigarette burns. No way had he just bought this thing at Home Depot.

Snoring at its base was a mammoth mountain of a dog.

"That's Rufus," Andre said, following my gaze.

Rufus looked up and yawned a yawn the size of a sinkhole, baring a set of mighty scary looking teeth.

"Don't worry," Andre assured me. "He doesn't bite. Except for that one time. And that Girl Scout was asking for it."

He plopped onto the sofa, sending up a small cloud of dust. "Have a seat," he said, gesturing to the armchair.

I sat down gingerly, careful to avoid an ominous brown stain at the edge.

"Wanna brownie?" he asked, pointing to a plate of misshapen brownies on the coffee table. Like the rest of the house, they reeked of marijuana.

"No, thanks," I said, for one of the few times in my life passing up chocolate.

"More for me," he said, grabbing one.

He broke off a tiny piece and tossed it to his megadog.

"Here you go, Rufus."

The dog roused himself from his stupor long enough to scarf it down. No wonder he was so zoned out.

"Are you sure it's healthy, feeding marijuana to a dog?"

"Oh, Rufus eats this stuff all the time, and he's just fine. Aren't you, Rufus?"

The dog snored in reply.

"So what do you wanna know?" he asked, eyes glued to the TV, where SpongeBob was doing battle with a piece of plankton.

"Your brother Raymond tells us he was with you the morning of Tommy LaSalle's murder."

"Yep," he nodded. "We were out buying a coffee-maker."

"Really? Raymond says you were buying a coffee table."

"Oh, right. Coffee table. Coffeemaker. I always get those two confused."

"So where is it?" I asked. "Your new coffee table?"

"It's around here somewhere. I haven't had a chance to assemble it yet."

"Mind if I take a look at it?"

The wheels spun ever so slowly in what passed for his brain before he answered.

"I just remembered. I loaned it to a friend. But I was with my brother that morning at Ikea, I swear."

"Really? Your brother said he was at Home Depot."

"Ikea. Home Depot. I always get those confused, too."

I was shaking my head in wonder that Raymond had trusted his alibi to his numbskull brother when there was a knock on the door.

Andre shuffled off to get it, his bare feet cracked with dirt at the heels.

Just as I was trying to decide which smelled worse—Rufus or the stench of marijuana—I heard someone at the door shout, "LAPD."

Oh, hell. It was the *real* police.

And I couldn't get caught impersonating a police officer. Not again.

(Yes, I've done it before. Sorry about that, Mom.)

Springing up from the armchair, I dashed over to a swinging door at the far end of the room and found myself in Andre's kitchen, a hellhole of a room with enough dishes in the sink to stock a small restaurant.

Thank heavens there was a back door. I vaulted over to it and turned the knob, only to realize it was dead-bolted shut. Dammit! I was trapped!

Then I looked down and saw it: a ginormous doggie door—large enough to accommodate Rufus.

Before you could say "Down, boy," I was on my knees, shoving myself past the filthy plastic flap to freedom. Or trying to, anyway. It was a mighty tight squeeze.

"Mildred Pierce?" I heard the real police officer saying. "There's nobody in Homicide by that name."

Ack! Any minute the police would come charging into the kitchen and find me with my fanny halfway out the doggie door.

With one last heroic attempt, I sucked in my gut and forced myself out of that filthy opening.

I landed on a tiny flagstone patio and blinked in amazement at what I saw. Aside from the patio, the entire backyard was covered with marijuana plants, some shooting up as high as five feet.

Frantically searching for an escape route, I groaned to see the yard was bordered by high fences on both sides, way too high to scale without a ladder and Kevlar panties.

Then I spotted my salvation: a gate at the rear of the yard.

Without wasting another second, I began hacking my way through the marijuana plants like Indiana Jones in a cannabis jungle.

I was almost at the gate when I tripped over a stray branch and went sprawling to the ground.

Why, today of all days, had I worn a brand new Eileen Fisher blouse? Now it was streaked with dirt.

But I didn't have time to worry about my ruined blouse. I picked myself up and charged ahead to the gate, which—praise be!—was unlocked. Shoving it open, I stepped out into an alley littered with trash.

A homeless man sat in front of an abandoned mattress, reading a rumpled copy of the *Los Angeles Times*.

He took one look at me and opened his mouth to speak.

Assuming he was going ask for money, I felt around in my purse for my wallet.

But he didn't want my money.

Instead, he reached into a plastic bag beside him and pulled out a bar of soap.

"Here, sweetheart," he said. "You need this more than I do."

It was then that I realized I reeked of Rufus and weed.

Blushing to the roots of my cannabis-infested hair, I declined his offer and made my way back to my Corolla, hoping I wouldn't run into the cops who'd come to question Andre.

The coast was clear when I got back out to the street.

So I sprinted to my car, stinking up a storm—and certain that whatever Raymond was doing the morning of the murder, he hadn't been doing it with his brother.

Chapter 24

Actually, I had a very good reason to wear my new Eileen Fisher blouse that day.

Those of you paying close attention to my little story and not running off to the fridge for snacks will no doubt recall that I'd promised to set up a date for Dickie and me to get together with Lance.

And today was the day. We'd agreed to meet up for a seven o'clock movie at the Century City Mall.

By the time I left Andre's it was a little after five, and I figured I had just enough time to stop off at my apartment for a quick shower and a bite to eat.

But I figured wrong. Very wrong.

The freeway had been bad enough when I drove down to Hawthorne, but now it was a nightmare on wheels, cars inching along at a snail's pace.

Correction. I'm sure there were plenty of snails at that moment making better time than we were.

No way was I going to be able to make it to my apartment. I'd be lucky if I made it in time for the movie.

When I finally pulled in the Century City parking lot, it was 7:02.

Wasting no time, I raced to the escalator—plucking a marijuana leaf from my hair en route—and hustled to the Cineplex, where Dickie and Lance were waiting for me outside the entrance.

Dickie looked cute as ever in jeans and a turtleneck; Lance, dressed to impress in a nosebleed-expensive designer sweater.

As I approached them I could hear Lance saying, "I just love your hair, Dickie. I saw the exact same style in a Supercuts ad."

"Hey, guys," I said, zipping over to join them before Lance could deliver another zinger. "I see you've already introduced yourselves."

"Yes," Lance said. "I recognized Dickie from your wedding album. In spite of the crossed eyes you drew on all his pictures."

"How's it going, sweetie?" Dickie said to me, ignoring Lance's thoughtful reminder of how miserable our marriage had been.

He reached out to give me a hug, but Lance slid in and beat him to it.

"Yes, sweetie, how's it going?" Then he wrinkled his nose in disgust. "PU! What have you been rolling around in?"

Damn. I'd opened the windows in my Corolla and was hoping all those freeway exhaust fumes had gotten rid of my eau de Rufus.

"You smell like weed and something really disgusting."

"Dog hair."

"Weed and dog hair? Ugh! I don't know whether to pet you or smoke you."

"You smell just fine," Dickie reassured me.

But I couldn't help notice how quickly he pulled back from the hug he'd started to give me.

"I'm so sorry I'm late."

"No problem," Dickie said. "The trailers run forever. We have plenty of time."

We made our way inside the Cineplex, and as we passed the snack bar, Dickie asked, "Can I get you some water, Jaine?"

"Hahaha!" Lance guffawed. "Are you kidding? The only time Jaine would ever order water at a movie was if the place was on fire. What'll you have, sweetie? Your usual Coke and jumbo Raisinets?"

"You know I don't eat sweets anymore, Lance," I said, shooting him a death ray glare. Then I turned back to Dickie. "Water will be great," I lied.

"Well, I'm starving," Lance said. "I'll get the Raisinets for me."

What a stinker. Lance never eats sweets in the movies. He was just buying them in the hopes I'd break down in front of Dickie and grab a handful.

Fully armed with waters and jumbo Raisinets, we headed into the theater to find our seats.

Dickie led the way to our row, and I was just about to follow him to our seats when Lance darted in front of me, practically shoving me aside so that he'd be sitting between Dickie and me.

"I want to sit next to Dickie," he said, "so I can get to know him better."

I plopped down in my seat, more than a tad irritated.

And by now I was starving. The last thing I'd eaten was that Dove Bar a zillion hours ago.

Lance popped a Raisinet in his mouth.

"Mmm, yummy."

The little sadist.

It was all I could do not to grab a bunch and inhale them. But somehow I restrained myself and just sucked on my calorie-free water.

As the previews for coming attractions started playing on the screen, I noticed two couples near us getting up and changing their seats.

"What's that awful smell?" I heard one woman mutter to her friend.

"Weed and dog hair!" Lance called out helpfully.

I wish I could tell you what movie we saw that night, but I can't. Because we didn't see it.

The movie hadn't even begun when we were approached by a beanpole of an usher. "I'm so sorry," he said, "but I'm going to have to ask you to leave. We've gotten several complaints about the . . . um . . . odor coming from you, ma'am," he added, nodding in my direction.

Omigosh, I was as bad as Daddy. Between the two of us, we were stinking up theaters from coast to coast.

"We'll refund your money, of course," the usher said as we got up from our seats.

"Lysol on seat G13," I heard him whisper to one of his colleagues on our way out of the theater.

All in all, a most humiliating experience.

Afterwards we agreed to meet up at my apartment,

where the first thing I did was excuse myself and leap in the shower, eager to wash away all traces of my romp in the marijuana patch.

As I tore off my clothes, Prozac looked up from where she was napping on my toilet tank and sniffed in disgust.

Yee-uck! I've been in litter boxes that smelled better than you.

When I was sparkle-clean and smelling of strawberry-scented shampoo, I hurried back to my bedroom and slipped into jeans and a sweatshirt.

I was hungrier than ever, but all I had in my kitchen were cold pizza and Oreos, and I couldn't possibly eat those in front of Dickie. Instead I searched through my handbags and pockets, looking for unfinished snacks.

Sadly all I came up with was a linty Life Saver and a few stray M&M's that had survived the spin class debacle. I scarfed them down in nanoseconds, and after gargling with Listerine to remove all traces of chocolate from my breath, I headed out to the living room.

There I found Lance cozying up to Dickie on the sofa, showing him pictures from his cell phone. Much to my consternation, I heard him saying:

"Wait'll you see this picture of Jaine eating ice cream with a soup ladle. It's hilarious! Oh, and here she is finishing off a banana cream pie!"

Racing over, I grabbed the phone from his hand.

"That's enough show and tell, Lance. Dickie already knows about my past as a junk food eater."

"I'm so proud of you for changing your ways," Dickie said, giving my hand a squeeze.

"Of course!" Lance said. "I keep forgetting you two were married. Which reminds me," he added, spreading out on his half of the sofa and forcing me to sit all by my lonesome on my chintz armchair, "I was reading an interesting article in the paper the other day. They did this study that tracked divorced couples who reconnected. More than eighty percent of them split up within a year."

What a royal crock. The only thing Lance ever read in the paper was his horoscope. Which brought him to Topic Number Two.

"So what's your astrological sign?" he asked Dickie.

"I don't believe in astrology. My guru says our lives are determined not by the stars, but by our souls."

"How insightful," Lance said with patently insincere sincerity. "But just for a minute, humor me. What's your sign?"

"Taurus."

Lance clucked in pity.

"Too bad. Jaine's a Leo. Totally incompatible! Not that it's necessarily true in your case. There are always exceptions to the rule. I'm sure you two will be just fine together," he added with a simpering smile.

"I'm so glad we have your vote of confidence," I snapped.

"Raisinet, anyone?" he asked, holding out the box, still hoping to lure me into stuffing my face in front of Dickie.

"I'm so sorry I can't offer you guys something to eat," I said, "but all I've got are some old martini olives."

"I'm fine," Dickie said. "I had a big salad before I met you guys."

"All these Raisinets have made me thirsty," Lance said, getting up from the sofa. "I'm going to get myself some water. You're not out of that, too, are you, Jaine?"

"No," I snarled, "my kitchen faucet's right where it's always been."

The minute the little ratfink was gone, I leaped over to the sofa and cuddled up next to Dickie.

"Well, hello, there," he said in his velvety foreplay voice.

Then he began nibbling my ear. Which almost made the whole miserable evening worthwhile.

"Sorry about Lance," I said, mid-nibble. "He's being a total jerk."

"He seems okay to me."

"Really?" I asked, taken aback.

"I try to find something good in everyone I meet."

"Yeah, well, you'd need an electronic microscope to find something good in Lance tonight."

Before I could trash him anymore, Mr. Impossible came tripping back into the living room.

"Guess what I found in Jaine's cupboard. Oreos!" He waved the package of cookies gleefully. "We've got snacks, after all!"

"Is that so?" I said, stifling the urge to ram one up his nose. "What with my new diet, I forgot I even had them."

"Well, here they are," Lance said, tossing them on the coffee table.

"None for me, thanks," Dickie said.

"Me either," I chimed in, stealing Lance's maneuver and kicking out my legs so there was absolutely no room for him on the sofa.

Which didn't seem to bother him a bit as he settled in my armchair with an Oreo.

"Yum!" he said, licking the crème from the center.

I was seriously thinking about ways to decapitate the duplicitous little toad when he cried, "Look who's here! My favorite cat!"

And indeed, I turned and saw Prozac prancing into the room, fresh from her nap on my toilet tank.

"Come here, princess, and sit with Uncle Lance!" Lance cooed.

He patted his knees, and before you could say Shameless Hussy, she was curled up in his lap.

"Jaine tells me you've been having trouble bonding with Prozac," Lance said to Dickie, oozing fake concern.

"Prozac's coming around," I said. "Before long, she'll be madly in love with him."

From her perch on Lance's lap, Prozac shot me an incredulous look.

As if.

"Funny," Lance said, scratching her behind her ears, "Prozac adores me."

The little turncoat looked up at him, goo-goo eyed.

"I always believe animals are such good judges of people's character."

Pro thumped her tail in approval.

Amen to that, brother!

"Although I'm sure she's wrong in your case, Dickie. . . . Naughty Prozac, you mustn't keep hissing at Dickie like that."

Dickie was smiling stiffly, but I could tell his determination to find the good in Lance was being severely tested.

Enough was enough.

"Lance," I said, glaring at him, "isn't it time for you to get going? Don't you have to get up early for work tomorrow?"

"Don't be silly. Neiman's doesn't open until ten. And besides, I've got the day off! I can stay as late as I want!"

Dickie blanched at this latest newsflash.

"Well," he said, getting up, "Lance may not have to get to work early tomorrow, but I do. I'd better be pushing off."

"Don't go!" I cried.

"No, don't!" Lance said. "I want to tell you about my customers at Neiman's. You wouldn't believe the bunions I've seen!"

"Sorry, I've got to run."

And, after a hurried peck on my cheek, he was gone.

The minute he left, I whirled on Lance, livid.

Okay, the minute he left, I stuffed my face with an Oreo.

Then I whirled on Lance.

"I may never speak to you again."

"Why?" he asked, all wide-eyed innocence, an act he no doubt picked up from Prozac.

"Don't pretend you don't know what a skunk you've been all night."

"Me?" Still playing innocent.

"You did your best to sabotage me. The Raisinets, the Oreos, the horoscope, the picture of me eating ice cream with a soup ladle, the stupid study about divorced couples reconnecting, reminding Dickie how much Prozac hates him—"

Over in the armchair, Prozac meowed.

He was right about that.

"Seriously, Lance. I'm furious. You need to leave. Now."

Suddenly he dropped the innocent act, a stricken look on his face.

"I'm so sorry, Jaine. You're right, I behaved abominably."

And then I saw something I'd never seen before:

Tears in his eyes.

In all the years I'd known Lance, he's been a major-league drama queen, but I'd never actually seen him cry.

"It's just that I'm so afraid of losing you," he said, gulping back a sob. "I keep thinking that you'll marry Dickie and move away and you'll be out of my life forever."

Now he was crying for real, and at the sight of all those tears, I felt my anger draining away.

"Don't be crazy, Lance. No matter what happens with Dickie, you and I will always be friends."

"Does that mean you've forgiven me for being such a rat tonight?"

"That depends."

"On what?"

"On whether you toss me the rest of the Oreos."

"Oh, Jaine!" He wrapped me in a big bear hug. "I really do love you."

"No, I was serious. Pass me those Oreos. I'm starving."

"I'll do better than that. I'll take you to dinner at your favorite restaurant, Obicà Mozzarella Bar."

That sealed it. We were BFFs again.

"And I was wrong about Dickie," Lance said, giving my hand a squeeze. "He seems like a really nice guy."

An indignant yowl from Prozac.

Traitor!

YOU'VE GOT MAIL!

To: Jausten
From: DaddyO
Subject: The High Road

Dearest Lambchop—I've decided to take the high road and forgive your mom for throwing out Big Al's styling wax. Clearly, she's still jealous of all the attention my hair has been getting.

And to show her there are no hard feelings, I'm taking her to Le Chateaubriand for dinner.

Love 'n hugs from
Your magnanimous,
DaddyO

PS. Can't wait to wow everyone at the restaurant with my hot new hairdo.

To: Jausten
From: Shoptillyoudrop
Subject: Darn It to Heck!

Darn it to heck! Daddy wants to show off his new haircut at Le Chateaubriand. Just the thought of being seen in public with his smelly do gives me the willies. But as you well know, Le Chateaubriand happens to be Tampa Vista's most exclusive restaurant, and I simply can't resist their molten chocolate lava cake.

Maybe, if I play my cards right, Daddy and I can sit at separate tables.

XOXO,
Mom

To: Jausten
From: Shoptillyoudrop
Subject: What a Fiasco!

Just got back from Le Chateaubriand. What a fiasco. The maître d' took one sniff of Daddy's smelly hair, and for a minute I thought he was going to refuse to seat us.

But there were plenty of tables available, so he was trapped. With great reluctance, he led us to a table as far from everyone else as possible. Clearly, he didn't want Daddy stinking up the room.

Once the busboy dropped off some rolls at our table and ran for cover, Daddy and I ordered chateaubriand for two, which usually tastes divine. But not tonight. Not with the cloud of rotting fish hanging over us.

Then, just when I thought things couldn't possibly get any worse, I looked up and saw the maître d' leading another couple over to our corner of the restaurant. By now the place was filling up and he had no choice but to sit people near us.

I almost fainted when I saw the couple. It was Harvy, our hair stylist, out to dinner with his wife.

I already told you how sensitive Harvy is and how furious he was with me for "cheating" on him at Supercuts. Well, my Supercut was nothing compared to Daddy's Haircut from Hell.

I lowered my eyes and prayed he wouldn't recognize us. But the next thing I heard was:

"My God, Hank! What did you do to your hair?"

"Got a new cut," Daddy grinned. "Isn't it great?"

"Oh, it's fabulous," Harvy said.

Anyone with half an ear could tell his voice was dripping with sarcasm, but not Daddy.

"That's seems to be the general consensus," Daddy crowed as Harvy stalked off, fuming.

I finished what was left of my steak, but my heart wasn't it. I kept wondering if Harvy would ever forgive Daddy and—even more important—hoping he wasn't mad at me, too.

Finally, when the waiter had cleared away our dinner plates, I mustered up my courage and headed over to talk to him.

"Harvy, dear," I said as I approached his table, "I'm so sorry Hank went to another salon."

"Where your husband chooses to get his hair cut is his business, not mine," Harvy sniffed, icy as could be.

"I certainly hope this doesn't affect our relationship," I said, with my most ingratiating smile. "I've been meaning to call to set up an appointment."

"I'm afraid I'm booked up for the next several months."

His wife looked at me, eyes full of pity.

Darn it all! I've just been excommunicated by the best stylist in Tampa Vistas, all because of Daddy!

XOXO from
Your furious,
Mom

PS. I was so upset by the end of the meal, I could hardly scrape the last of the molten chocolate lava from my plate.

To: Jausten
From: DaddyO
Subject: Harvy Loves It!

Just got back from Le Chateaubriand, Lambchop, where the maître d', clearly impressed by my new look, gave us the VIP treatment—seating us in a secluded romantic nook. What's more, Harvy, the guy who normally cuts my hair, stopped by our table and told me my new cut looked fabulous.

Love 'n snuggles from,
DaddyO

Chapter 25

The day of Tommy's burial at sea dawned bright and sunny.

If he were still alive, he'd have been at the pool working on his tan.

Daisy had me book a whoppingly expensive 100-foot yacht for the occasion, a gleaming teak and brass beauty complete with lounging salon, three bedrooms, and a kitchen—not to mention a captain and crew.

"I know it seems extravagant," she said of the $5,000 price tag, "but I want to send Tommy off in style."

And so, at one o'clock that afternoon, I was seated out on the deck of the yacht with Daisy and my fellow celebrants—I mean, mourners—waiting for the captain to get clearance to set sail.

Daisy sat with Clayton and Esme on a plush white leather banquette on one side of the deck, while Raymond, Solange, and I sat across from them in equally plush armchairs.

Propped up on a table between us was an urn containing Tommy's ashes, alongside a framed photo of the dearly departed, smiling the same oily smile he'd been smirking the first day I met him.

Daisy had invited Raymond and Solange as guests—not hired help—in recognition of all the extra work they'd done for Tommy. That's what she said, anyway. I suspect she just wanted more mourners at the ceremony.

We'd all been urged not to wear black; Daisy wanted the memorial to be "as bright and festive as Tommy."

And indeed Daisy was clad in a turquoise pantsuit, accessorized with a pair of beautiful turquoise drop earrings Tommy had "given" her—no doubt courtesy of Daisy's credit card.

So there we were, sipping champagne that was meant for the wedding and chomping down on the kind of delicate "sissy food" Tommy would have hated—avocado toast, mini quiches, mushroom-gruyere flatbread, and caviar with crème fraîche.

I glanced over at Tommy's photo, and for the briefest instant, I swear his smile turned into a scowl. I could almost hear him whining, *Where's the beef jerky?*

I was busy inhaling some avocado toast, and wondering if Mom would ever worm her way back into Harvy's good graces, when one of the yacht's stewards approached.

"Excuse me, ma'am," he said to Daisy. "Another guest has arrived."

"Another guest?" Daisy blinked, surprised. "I didn't invite any other guests."

Then the mystery guest came into view.

It was Kate, holding a large bouquet of daisies.

I'd spoken with her earlier in the week and mentioned the burial, but had no idea she'd actually show up.

Daisy stiffened at the sight of her

"Hello, Daisy," Kate said with a tentative smile. "I came to pay my respects."

Daisy remained ramrod straight.

"Is that so? Perhaps you should've shown some of that respect to Tommy when he was alive. I know all about your horrible voodoo doll."

Kate blushed.

"Forgive me, Daisy. I was under a lot of stress. You know I'd never do anything to upset you."

"I'm sorry," Daisy said, "but until I'm certain you didn't kill Tommy, there's no place for you in my life—or on this boat. I'm afraid you're going to have to leave."

She looked around for the crewman, but he was nowhere in sight.

"Jaine, dear," Daisy said, turning to me, "please show Kate off the boat."

Grabbing another hors d'oeuvre for the road, I got up and escorted Kate to the gangplank, grateful to have a chance to chat with her.

"Damn," she said when we were out of earshot of the others. "I was hoping Daisy would have forgiven me by now. It's impossible lining up work without a reference."

"Here," I said. "Have some avocado toast. That'll make you feel better."

"Thanks," she said, scarfing it down.

Like me, Kate was never too depressed to eat.

"So how's it going with your investigation?" she asked, a misplaced glimmer of hope in her eyes.

"About the same as it was the last time we spoke.

Plenty of suspects. No evidence. Although I managed to bust Raymond's alibi yesterday."

"Really?"

"He wasn't with his brother at Home Depot like he claimed, but that's no proof he killed Tommy."

"Well, keep trying. Any minute now, I'll probably be a friendly neighborhood Uber driver. And I won't even get that gig if they find out I'm a suspect in Tommy's murder."

Brimming with guilt for not having made more progress, I promised to do my best to unearth Tommy's killer. Then we hugged good-bye and Kate walked down the gangplank, shoulders slumped, the bouquet of daisies limp in her arms.

I was on my way back to join the mourners when I saw Raymond and Solange standing together at the yacht's railing, out of view of the others.

"Hey, Jaine," Raymond said, spotting me. "You're just in time. Solange and I are going to have our own private burial at sea."

With that, Solange reached into her purse and took out a jumbo-sized bag of Tater Tots.

"May I never look at another one of these as long as I live," Raymond said, tossing them overboard.

"And may I never look at a pair of these!" Solange said, hurling a pair of Tommy's thongs into the sea.

"Adios, Tommy!" they giggled.

Once again, I was reminded of how much they hated Tommy, and how much they stood to gain from his death.

It took us more than an hour to get to Malibu, during which time the champagne was flowing. And flowing. By the time we reached the waters below Tommy's favorite restaurant, most of the mourners were pretty well sloshed.

Only Daisy seemed on the sober side of a DUI.

So when she asked everyone to say a little something about the dearly departed, I shuddered to think of what they'd say.

"Scheming sociopath" and "selfish bastard" were words that came to mind.

But fortunately everyone managed to rein in their true thoughts.

"I can honestly say I never met anyone quite like him," Raymond said.

"Yes, he was certainly one of a kind," Solange echoed.

"I loved the chili cheese dogs he ordered from Pink's" was the best I could do.

When it was her turn, Esme launched into a highly fictional ode to Tommy, babbling on about what a kind, spirited, fun-loving lad he'd been, "a joyous burst of energy in our humdrum lives."

Never had I heard so much bilge pour out of one woman's mouth.

We all listened to her, trying to control our gag reflexes. Everyone except Daisy, of course, who smiled at Esme gratefully.

When Esme finally wrapped up her spiel, it was Clayton's turn to speak.

Clad in khakis and a blue blazer, his silver hair glinting in the sun, he looked every inch the yachtsman as he took Daisy's hand in his.

I flashed back to that tennis match where Tommy had humiliated him so badly, and the look of utter loathing in Clayton's eyes when he'd conceded defeat to his rival.

Clayton had clearly detested Tommy, but now those

feelings were tucked away out of sight as he smiled lovingly at Daisy.

"I liked that he made you happy, Daisy."

"Oh, Clayton!" she cried. "That's so very kind of you."

She gazed at him with newfound appreciation and gave his hand a squeeze. Well played, Clayton!

Daisy's eulogy was short and heartfelt.

"I'm afraid if I talk too much, I'll start to cry. All I can say is that Tommy brought me a great deal of happiness and I shall never forget him."

This was it. The big moment. Time for Tommy to swim with the fishes.

Daisy picked up the urn and gazed at it, eyes brimming with tears. Then she brought it to her lips and kissed it. Taking a deep breath, she pried the lid open and flung Tommy's ashes into the sea.

Behind me, I could hear Solange whisper to Raymond, "I thought he'd never leave."

As Tommy's ashes hit the water, the sun disappeared behind a cloud.

The ocean suddenly seemed dark and brooding, as if saying, *What's HE doing here?*

Daisy, who'd kept it together up until this point, began crying softly.

"There, there," Esme said, clutching Daisy to her flat bosom. "You mustn't cry. Esme's here."

Clayton hurriedly reached into his pocket for a handkerchief, and as he did, a small slip of paper fluttered to the floor.

But Clayton didn't notice, caught up as he was in wiping away Daisy's tears.

I bent down to pick it up and saw it was a credit card receipt.

Something—call it my part-time, semi-professional sleuthing instinct—made me slip it in my purse.

And I was mighty glad I did.

Because the minute I'd excused myself to use the restroom, I took a closer look at it and saw that it was a restaurant receipt in Clayton's name from the Bel Air Bar & Grill.

And here's where it gets really interesting.

The receipt was dated the day of Tommy's murder.

So Clayton hadn't been visiting his son in Carmel, after all.

He'd been right here in Los Angeles, within easy stabbing distance of Tommy.

Chapter 26

It was definitely time for a chat with the neighborhood tennis ace.

The next day I took a break from the turquoise mines and trotted down the street to his house.

Not nearly as elaborate as Daisy's place, it was still an impressive piece of 1920s Tudor architecture, with beveled glass windows and wood beams crisscrossing the stucco exterior.

I rang the bell, setting off a series of mellifluous chimes.

The door was quickly opened by Clayton's valet, Marco—the same hulking guy who'd stopped off at La Belle Vie the day of the murder with a wedding gift.

"May I help you?" he asked.

With his beefy frame filling the doorway, he looked more like a professional wrestler than a butler in Bel Air.

"Hi, I'm Jaine Austen. We met at Daisy's house."

"Right," he said, nodding. "I remember."

"I was hoping to speak with Mr. Manning."

"He's in the den. Let me tell him you're here."

He ushered me into the foyer, where I waited next to a potted fern and a framed oil painting of Clayton in his tennis whites.

Soon Marco was back.

"Right this way," he said, leading me down a corridor.

He opened the door to a spacious den, where Clayton was seated on a sectional sofa, playing a video game on a wall-mounted TV. Another wall, I noticed, was chock-ablock with photos.

Clayton jumped up to greet me, pausing his video game and beaming me his courtly smile as Marco drifted out of the room.

"How nice to see you, Jaine."

"Hope I'm not interrupting.

"No, no. Just playing a little video tennis."

He gestured to the TV screen, where athletic avatars were frozen mid-game. Why did I get the feeling this was where Clayton scored most of his tennis victories?

"That's my family," he said, following my gaze as I turned to look at the wall filled with photos. "My late wife." He pointed to several pictures of a motherly gal with a distinct resemblance to Daisy.

Who says men don't choose the same woman over and over again?

"And here are my kids, my grandkids, my great-grandkids. Oh, here I am with Andre Agassi. Terrific guy. And John McEnroe. Don't believe what you've read about him. A real softie. I actually gave him a few tips on how to improve his game."

Ouch. I could just imagine how well that must have gone over.

"Have a seat," he said, gesturing to the sofa.

"I have something I need to return to you," I said, perching kitty-corner from him on the sectional. Then I handed him the receipt from the Bel Air Bar & Grill, which I'd prudently copied on Daisy's printer. "You dropped this on the yacht yesterday."

"Bel Air Bar & Grill," he said, tossing the receipt on the coffee table in front of us. "Love that place. They make a damn good martini. Beefeater gin. Forget all these fancy new gins. There'll never be another gin as good as Beefeater."

Time to take a detour from martini lane.

"I couldn't help but notice the date on the receipt," I said.

"The date?" He blinked, puzzled.

"It seems you were there the day of Tommy's murder."

"So? What of it?"

"Marco stopped by La Belle Vie that day and said you were out of town visiting your son in Carmel."

"Oh, that," he said, waving away his presence in L.A. "A little fib I made up so I wouldn't have to be near the happy couple. Frankly, I was appalled when Daisy announced her engagement to that lowlife piece of trash. No way was I going to the wedding."

"Which meant you were here in Bel Air the day of the murder."

"Yes, but I had nothing to do with Tommy's death, if that's what you're implying."

"Not implying. Just wondering."

A look of annoyance flitted across his face.

"Esme told me you were snooping around asking

questions about the murder. Good riddance to bad rub-
bish, but I'm not the one who took Tommy out."

"Any idea who might have done it?"

"Kate, of course. Esme saw her going into the gym."

"Anyone other than Kate?"

"Why are you so sure she didn't do it?"

"I worked side by side with her, and I don't believe
she's capable of murder. This accusation hanging over
her head is ruining her life. If you can think of anything
that might help clear her name, I'd really appreciate it."

He hesitated a beat before he replied.

"I'm sure it's nothing," he said, squirming uncomfort-
ably on the sofa. "But Esme once mentioned something
about hiring a hit man to do away with Tommy. At the
time I thought she was kidding. And I still do. But there's
always the remote possibility she meant it."

At which point there was a knock on the door, and
Marco entered, bearing Clayton's lunch on a tray. Triple-
decker club sandwich bursting with ham and turkey. With
a side of curly fries.

"If you'll excuse me," Clayton said, "my lunch is ready
and I'm in the middle of a very important match."

He nodded at the avatars on the screen.

"Show Ms. Austen out, will you, Marco?" he said, his
smile a heck of a lot chillier than it had been when I first
showed up.

I thanked him for his time and followed Marco out of
the room.

As we headed to the foyer, Marco started talking about
what a great guy Clayton was and how much he enjoyed
working for him. But I wasn't really paying attention,
distracted by what Clayton had said about Esme (not to
mention those curly fries).

Was it possible Esme hired a hit man to bump off Tommy? Had she tiptoed out of the living room the morning of the murder to let in her murderous accomplice? And then pointed an accusing finger at Kate to draw suspicion away from herself?

I was lost in my thoughts when I heard Marco saying, "I'll always be grateful to Mr. Manning for saving my life."

"Clayton saved your life?" I asked, snapping to attention.

"He hired me when no one else would. I'm a convicted felon. Did time in prison for grand theft auto when I was a kid. When I got out, I was a mess. Screwed up my life with a series of bad marriages and dead end jobs. And booze. Way too much booze. I was on the skids, one step away from cirrhosis of the liver, when Mr. Clayton took a chance on me and hired me to be his butler. He literally saved my life."

His eyes shone with gratitude.

"There isn't anything I wouldn't do for that man."

Anything?

And suddenly it occurred to me: Maybe it wasn't Esme who'd used a hit man to bump off Tommy. Maybe it was *Clayton*.

I flashed back to the morning of the murder, when Marco showed up with Clayton's wedding present. He'd asked if he could use the restroom and said he'd let himself out. What if, before leaving, he'd paid a quick trip to the gym to bump off his employer's detested nemesis?

A convicted felon, Marco was no stranger to crime. And he just said he'd do anything for Clayton.

Now I wondered if that included murder.

Chapter 27

I got back to La Belle Vie just in time to join Daisy and Esme for lunch out on the patio.

Daisy was pale and wan in a turquoise jog suit. Whatever energy she'd shored up for scattering Tommy's ashes at sea had been leeched out of her.

"Hello, Jaine," she greeted me absently, no doubt lost in thoughts of her beastly beloved.

"Don't sit there!" she cried out as I started to take a seat. "That's where Tommy used to sit. I know it's foolish, but for the time being, I'd rather no one else sit there."

"I totally understand," I lied, moving to another chair and hoping Daisy hadn't gone round the bend in her grief.

Somehow she managed a faint smile when Solange wheeled out our lunch.

"How lovely," she said, eyeing the shrimp scampi

swimming in garlic butter that Raymond had whipped up for our dining pleasure.

"Divine!" Esme exclaimed, pouncing on the stuff the minute her plate hit the table. "My compliments to Raymond!"

Daisy proceeded to pick at her food while Esme and I scarfed ours down with gusto.

Compared to Daisy, Esme was the picture of health, bright-eyed and beaming, salt-and-pepper hair particularly puffy under its helmet of hair spray. She'd probably be doing a jig on the table if she didn't have to fake mourning Tommy's death.

"Where's Clayton?" she asked between scampi bites.

"He's busy with an important tennis match," Daisy said. "He's such a talented player."

With a joystick, maybe. With a tennis racket, not so much.

"He's stopping by tonight to take me to dinner. I'm not really in the mood to go, but Clayton says I need to get out more."

"How right he is!" Esme enthused. "Which is why I wanted you to see this." She reached into her tote and took out a glossy brochure. "A twenty-one-day cruise to Tahiti. On Crystal Cruise Lines!"

Crystal? Only one of the most expensive barges tootling around the seven seas.

"I don't know," Daisy said, listlessly flipping through the brochure. "I doubt I'd be very good company."

"But you have to get away from all these memories. A change of scenery is just what you need."

Daisy thought this over, then forced a smile.

"You're right, Esme. It does sound like a good idea."

I remembered our chat after Tommy's death and Daisy's steely determination not to let it destroy her.

"But I'll only go if you come with me. My treat, of course."

"Anything you want, Daisy, darling," Esme cooed.

A free luxury cruise for Esme. Yep, life was sweet now that Tommy was out of the picture. She was sopping up her scampi butter with a sourdough roll when Solange came out to the patio.

"Phone call for you, Ms. Kincaid. From the UCLA School of Business."

"That must be about the scholarship I'm setting up in Tommy's name," Daisy said, scraping back her chair. "He had such a comprehensive grasp of the financial world."

Wow, somebody was still drinking the Tommy Kool-Aid.

Daisy followed Solange back into the house, leaving me alone with Esme.

Just the opportunity I'd been waiting for.

The more I thought about it, the more implausible it seemed that Esme hired a hit man to kill Tommy. Hit men cost big bucks, and Esme didn't have that kind of money. Or any kind of money, for that matter.

But I hadn't forgotten what she'd said at our last meeting. Namely, that she'd known about Tommy's snake tattoo—something she would have been aware of only if she'd seen him in his thongs at the gym.

Perhaps right before plunging a Swiss Army Knife in his neck.

I tore myself away from my one remaining shrimp, eager to question her before Daisy returned.

"So, how's everything going, Esme?"

"Much better than the last time we spoke. Daisy's re-instated her contributions to the Bel Air Animal Welfare League."

Having demolished all her shrimp, she now reached over and plucked one of Daisy's.

What the what? I thought, my jaw dropping just a tad. I've been known to nab an extra cookie or three in times of crisis but never off someone's plate without their permission.

"She won't miss it," Esme said, off my look of disbelief. "Daisy's eating like a bird these days. Anyhow, I hope I can still count on you not to say anything to her about my tiny bookkeeping irregularities."

Tiny bookkeeping irregularities? That's like calling the Grand Canyon a pothole.

"No, I won't say anything," I assured her, only because I didn't want to upset Daisy. "But I did want to talk to you about something else."

"Oh?" Eyebrows arched. "What's that?"

"When we last spoke, you mentioned a snake tattoo on Tommy's upper thigh. I never knew about it until I saw him lying dead in the gym. He never wore briefs at the pool. Only boxers. I was wondering how you knew about the tattoo, unless you'd seen him in the gym the morning of the murder."

She looked up from her purloined scampi and zapped me with a steely glare.

"Of course I saw his tattoo. Didn't you ever notice the way that thug sat, with his legs spread, flaunting himself like a stud on a porno site? All you had to do was look, and you could see everything. And I mean everything!"

She bristled in disgust.

I nodded as if I believed her, but I had my doubts.

Maybe because I'd seen Tommy plenty of times at the pool and never noticed anything X-rated.

Or maybe because the scampi-nabbing Esme was lying through her teeth.

Chapter 28

All you romance fans are probably wondering what happened with Dickie after you last saw him scooting out of my apartment.

Not much, I'm afraid.

I hadn't seen him since that god-awful movie date with Lance. He claimed he was busy working overtime at his ad agency. But, my paranoia having kicked in, I was certain he was cooling off on our relationship.

Which is why I was overjoyed when he called me after lunch and asked me to meet him at a Hapi-ness workshop in Hollywood that night.

True, I hated Hapi's no fat/no fun diet and inwardly rolled my eyes at his cornball affirmations. But I couldn't deny the fact that his beloved guru had helped Dickie turn his life around.

And so I eagerly agreed to join him at the workshop.

"See you there at six," Dickie said, after he'd given me Hapi's address.

"Wonderful!"

"I hope you read the pamphlet I sent you—about the Hapi Way of Life?"

"Absolutely," I fibbed.

Hadn't read a word of it. Nary a syllable. When it showed up in the mail weeks ago, I'd tossed it on my pile of unpaid bills and hadn't looked at it since.

I made a mental note to fish it out and read it ASAP, then spent the rest of the afternoon with C. Weatherly (who by now was having the raging warmies for Max Laredo, her studly turquoise miner).

I was just wrapping up a scene where Clarissa trips over a hunk of turquoise and Max catches her in his brawny arms, sending Clarissa's pulse skyrocketing, when I checked the time and realized it was after five. Leaving my plucky heroine in the throes of lust, I set out for the Hapi-ness workshop.

Crosstown traffic was its usual hellish mess, but I managed to make it there on the dot of six.

As I pulled up to the address Dickie had given me, I got my first glimpse of Hapi House: a rundown clapboard bungalow festooned with Japanese lanterns. I was about to head into the driveway when I saw a big DON'T EVEN THINK OF PARKING HERE sign on the gate.

Which, I must say, was a tad churlish for a guy who was supposed to be spreading sweetness and light, n'est-ce pas?

After an extremely frustrating search, I finally found a parking spot five blocks away. Which is why I showed up for the workshop fifteen minutes late, breathless and sweating like a turquoise miner.

The front door was open, so I let myself into the living room, where about a dozen people were seated cross-legged in a circle, eyes closed, chanting:

Today in every way I am getting happier and happier.

Scanning the group, I spotted Dickie in sweatpants and an ab-hugging tank top, which was all I really needed to get happier and happier.

A moon-faced guy with a shaved head, swathed in a white, gauzy robe, sat raised above the others on a platform.

I figured this had to be Hapi.

His deep brown skin meant he was either of the Indian persuasion or a spray tan fanatic. I couldn't help noticing the esteemed guru was seated on a comfy pillow, while the rest of the gang sat on the scuffed wooden floor.

I stood there, waiting until Hapi called an end to the chanting and gave everyone permission to open their eyes.

"Ah, welcome," he said, catching sight of me. "You must be Dickie's friend, Jaine."

Dickie waved and scooched over to make room for me next to him in the circle.

I was relieved to see that the gals here were a lot less gorgeous than the stunners at spin class. Most were pasty-faced women with limp, stringy hair. Which is what happens when you go on a diet that eliminates the all-important Chunky Monkey/Oreo food group.

As I settled down next to him, Dickie beamed me his sexy smile, and I breathed a sigh of relief. That disastrous night with Lance hadn't cooled him on our relationship after all.

"Now we're all going to close our eyes and go to our

inner happy places," Hapi said. "A serene, comfortable haven, where all is calm and stress-free—be it the beach at sunset, a bubbling brook, a cozy fire on a winter's afternoon. Whatever brings you joy."

I had no trouble whatsoever finding my happy place—Domino's, where I was soon lost in a reverie of a mushroom and sausage pizza dripping with cheese.

Frankly, I was a bit peckish, having had nothing to eat since those five scampi at lunch.

(Okay, six scampi. Following Esme's shameful example, I'd grabbed one of Daisy's shrimp from her plate.)

Back in my reverie, I'd polished off my pizza and was now scarfing down some Chunky Monkey. Hapi was right. This meditation thing was really quite relaxing.

So relaxing, in fact, that before I knew it I'd dozed off. Which I realized when I felt Dickie jabbing me awake with his elbow.

"You were snoring," he whispered in my ear.

Oh, Lord. How embarrassing.

Next to me, one of the pasty-faced gals tsked in disapproval.

But at least Hapi hadn't noticed. He sat on his pillow, eyes closed, lost in meditation.

Afraid I'd drift off and start snoring again, I kept my eyes open as the others continued to meditate. There I sat, wishing I'd grabbed a snack before I left La Belle Vie and wondering if there was a Domino's nearby, when out of the corner of my eye I noticed something crawling across the room.

Taking a closer look, I realized it was a beetle. And not just any beetle. This thing was humungous, the Mike Tyson of beetles.

And it was crawling right toward me.

With a screeching yelp, I whipped off one of my sneakers and whacked the critter to oblivion.

Everyone's eyes sprang open.

"Omigosh!" cried one of the Hapi campers, gasping in horror at the dead bug.

"I know," I said. "Isn't it the ickiest thing you've ever seen?"

"You've killed it!" another camper moaned.

"No need to thank me," I said, modestly. "Although I'd strongly recommend getting an exterminator out here ASAP."

You'd think they'd all be grateful, but no, they just stared at me, horror-struck.

"You killed Cleopatra," Hapi said, a sickly cast spreading across his deep tan.

"No, no. Cleopatra's been dead thousands of years. I killed a bug. That's all."

"I thought you said you read the Hapi-ness pamphlet," Dickie whispered in my ear. "Didn't you see the part about how Hapi and his followers, like the ancient Egyptians, believe that beetles are holy? Cleopatra was Hapi's prized possession."

Oh, hell! I'd just killed Hapi's holy beetle!

Looking up, I saw the shiny-pated guru giving me the stink eye.

"Don't be angry," he said to his flock with forced calm, the veins in his temple throbbing with a vengeance. "Our visitor didn't realize what she was doing. Everyone, repeat after me:

I find the good in everyone I meet, even if she happens to be a complete nincompoop.

Okay, so he left off the nincompoop part, but I knew damn well he was thinking it.

The veins in his temple still throbbing, Hapi adjourned the meeting early while one of the faithful scooped up Cleopatra's remains.

Suffice it to say, I wasn't going to be winning the Hapi House Miss Congeniality award.

"Can you ever forgive me?" I asked Dickie as we left Hapi's bungalow and made our way to the street.

"Of course, Jaine. Forgiveness is a cornerstone of the Hapi way of life. Now come here," he said, leading me to his car. "I have something for you."

I perked up, hoping it was something along the lines of a smooch.

But when we got to his car, an impressive BMW convertible, he didn't wrap me in his arms. Instead he popped open his trunk and took out a pale blue crystal.

"It's a creative energy crystal," he said. "I thought it would help you with your book."

Awww. Was he the sweetest guy ever, or what?

Here I'd just killed Hapi's holy beetle, and he wanted to help me with my book.

"Oh, Dickie," I cried, throwing my arms around his neck. "You're the best."

I waited for him to return my ardor, much like Max Laredo did with Clarissa Weatherly, and engulf me in a fiery kiss.

But all I got was a chaste peck on my forehead.

"Maybe I could come over to your place for a while," I suggested, eager to find my happy place with some transcendental whoopsie doodle.

"Sorry, hon. But I've got to get back to work. It's really a madhouse at the agency."

He walked me to my car, a stilted silence between us.

"Good night, Jaine," he said when we got to my Corolla.

Another antiseptic peck on my forehead.

I got in my car and started home, my paranoia back in full throttle, worried that Dickie hadn't really forgiven me for killing Cleopatra.

Maybe he wasn't going back to work.

Maybe he was headed to his condo to gaze at the photo of his old girlfriend and rue the day he ever broke up with her.

Chapter 29

Driving back to my apartment, I vowed to read the Hapi-ness pamphlet the minute I got home.

Well, not the minute I got home.

The minute I got home I ordered a mushroom and sausage pizza.

Then I fished out the pamphlet from my stack of unpaid bills.

But one look at Hapi's smiling face brought back memories of poor squished Cleopatra, and I just couldn't do it. Instead I shoved the pamphlet in my purse, promising myself I'd read it tomorrow at work.

Right then all I wanted was to wash the day away with a quick shower before the pizza guy showed up.

I hurried to the bathroom and turned on the shower, then started for my bedroom to tear off my clothes. But I hadn't taken two steps when I heard a thunderous crash in the bathroom.

Racing over, I opened the shower door and saw my heavy steel showerhead on the floor. Somehow it had come loose. Yikes! I could have been seriously—maybe even fatally—injured if I'd been standing underneath it.

With trembling hands, I turned off the hot water and stood there staring at the showerhead.

How on earth had it come loose?

I often move the showerhead around to spray the walls when I'm cleaning. Had I somehow loosened it in the process?

Or had someone loosened it for me?

Had the killer been following me, biding his or her time until I was away from my apartment, and then sneaked in to tamper with my showerhead?

Frantically I began running around my apartment, looking for signs of forced entry. But I found nothing. No broken windows, jimmied locks, or loosened screens.

My apartment was sealed tight as a drum.

I checked to see if Prozac was upset, but she was stretched out on the sofa, snoring like a buzz saw, having one of her seventeen daily naps.

Flooded with relief, I sank down next to her.

No one had broken into my apartment. No one was out to kill me. I must have unwittingly loosened the shower-head by myself.

I was leaning back into the sofa cushions, feeling my blood pressure drift down from the stratosphere, when Ahmad showed up with my pizza.

Yes, I'm on a first name basis with my pizza delivery guy.

It's how I roll.

After tipping him generously (his is a noble calling), I hurried to the kitchen with my gooey treasure. I opened the box, salivating over the chunks of mushroom and sausage swimming in a sea of cheese.

Eagerly, I cut myself a slice. But just as I was raising it to my lips, I was struck by a frightening thought.

The killer hadn't forced his or her way into my apartment. But what if they'd found the spare key I keep hidden under the geranium flowerpot by my front door and used it to let themselves in? Even worse, what if they kept the key and were coming back to finish me off for good?

Oh, Lord! If only I had Daisy's panic room to escape to!

My heart pounding, I abandoned my pizza and raced outside. Slowly I lifted the flowerpot, afraid of what I might find. But the key was still there, exactly where I left it under the pot.

Or—I suddenly wondered, a frisson of fear running down my spine—was the key a bit off to the side? Had it been moved just a tad?

"Jaine, are you okay?"

So engrossed had I been in thoughts of a deadly stalker that I hadn't heard Lance come up the path.

"I'm fine," I lied. "Just wondering, though, if you happened to notice anyone suspicious outside my apartment today?"

"No. I was at work all day, then met an Internet date for a drink. Ugh!" he groaned, "what a nightmare that was. But why do you ask?"

So far, I hadn't told Lance about Tommy's murder, or my attempts to clear Kate's name, hoping to avoid a lecture on the dangers of trying to track down cold-blooded killers without a gun or any professional training.

But now, feeling particularly vulnerable, I caved and told him everything.

"I'm afraid someone may have broken into my apartment and tampered with my showerhead."

"Jaine, Jaine, Jaine!" he tsked. "How many times have I warned you not to go chasing after homicidal maniacs?"

Oh, hell. I was about to get another lecture.

But just as Lance was about to launch his spiel, he stopped and sniffed.

"Is that pizza I smell?"

"Sausage and mushroom," I nodded.

"Great! I'm starving!" he said, racing into my apartment and making a beeline for the kitchen.

On the plus side, I was off the hook for that lecture.

On the minus side, I was out half a pizza.

I spent the next twenty minutes watching Lance inhale my pizza, all the while giving me a blow-by-blow account of his Internet date from hell.

"I couldn't get a word in edgewise," he said, not letting me get a word in edgewise. "I nursed my glass of pinot until I finally pretended I had an emergency root canal and made my escape.

"Oh, Jaine," he sighed. "You don't know how lucky you are to have found Dickie."

"Yeah, right," I said, taking a desultory bite of pizza, wondering if I'd ever see Dickie again.

At last Lance ran out of steam (and pizza) and bid me good night.

"Try not to worry, hon," he said, scarfing down a final piece of crust. "I'm sure nobody broke into your apartment today."

"You really think that?" I asked hopefully.

"Absolutely. But just in case, sleep with a can of mace under your pillow. And remember, I'm right next door if you need me. Just bang on the wall. But not before ten in the morning. I'm sleeping in tomorrow."

And off he scooted into the night.

After retrieving my key from under the flowerpot, I headed to the bathroom for a nice long soak in the tub.

No way was I going near my shower in the foreseeable future.

YOU'VE GOT MAIL!

To: Jausten
From: DaddyO
Subject: An Artistic Triumph!

Exciting news, Lambchop!

We just got our sculptures back from the kiln, and I'm proud to say my Statue of Liberty is an artistic triumph! So much better than The Battle-Ax's stupid torso of Sir Isaac "Fig" Newton. While technically proficient, Sir Isaac lacks the creative spark that radiates from my Lady Liberty.

I've put it on the fireplace mantel, where it's sure to be admired by everyone who sees it.

Love 'n hugs
From your very proud,
DaddyO

To: Jausten
From: Shoptillyoudrop
Subject: Gummy Bear with a Torch

Just got our sculptures back. I'm afraid my canape plate turned out a tad bumpy, but I'm sure no one will notice the bumps once you've got canapes on it. I'll ship it out to you ASAP!

Daddy's convinced himself his Statue of Liberty is the greatest piece of art to come down the pike since the Mona Lisa. But if you ask me, it looks like a gummy bear with a torch.

He's got it up on the mantel, an eyesore for all to see. But it won't be there for long, not if I have anything to say about it.

Meanwhile, Lydia's bust of Sir Isaac Newton turned out beautifully. Lydia captured Sir Isaac's prominent nose and long wavy hair to a T. She's such a talented woman!

Must run and move Daddy's Statue of Liberty to a less conspicuous place on the mantel.

XOXO,
Mom

To: Jausten
From: Shoptillyoudrop
Subject: Oh, My Stars!

Oh, my stars! Guess what I just saw on the *Tampa Vistas Gazette* website: A photo of Lydia's statue of Sir Isaac Newton! It turns out that Molly, our instructor, loves it so much, she's going to exhibit it in her art gallery in a Grand Unveiling Ceremony!

Isn't that simply thrilling?

XOXO,
Mom

To: Jausten
From: DaddyO
Subject: Gross Miscarriage of Justice

Would you believe our idiotic sculpting instructor has chosen to exhibit The Battle-Ax's torso of "Fig" Newton at her art gallery?

Up to now I thought Molly was a woman of discerning taste. How wrong I was. I can't believe she overlooked my mesmerizing Statue of Liberty in favor of The Battle-Ax's lump of clay.

What a gross miscarriage of justice!

Even worse, there's going to be a gala Unveiling Ceremony at the gallery. Your mom says I'll look like a sore loser if I don't go, but I don't care. No way am I going to that gala. And nothing, but nothing, will make me change my mind!

Love 'n snuggles from,
DaddyO

To: Jausten
From: Shoptillyoudrop
Subject: Temper Tantrum

Daddy, in one of his temper tantrums, is refusing to go to the Grand Unveiling of Lydia's statue. Frankly, I'm relieved. The last thing I need is Daddy pouting at my side all night.

XOXO,
Mom

To: Jausten
From: DaddyO
Subject: Change of Heart

Guess what, Lambchop? I've decided to go to the Grand Unveiling. After careful consideration, I decided Mom was right. I don't want to look like a sore loser.

To: Jausten
From: Shoptillyoudrop
Subject: Drat!

Oh, drat. Daddy's coming to the Grand Unveiling. He says he wants to be a good sport. But the only reason he changed his mind is because he found out there's going to be a free buffet. You know Daddy. He can never resist the lure of free food!

XOXO,
Mom

To: Jausten
From: DaddyO
Subject: Justice Will Be Served!

Dearest Lambchop—I just figured out a great way to give my Statue of Liberty the exposure it deserves! Will fill you in on the details later.

All I can say for now is that artistic justice, at long last, will be served.

Love 'n snuggles from,
DaddyO

Chapter 30

First thing the next morning, I called a locksmith and had my lock changed.

I tried to convince myself that I'd overreacted to the showerhead incident, that I'd undoubtedly loosened it myself. But I couldn't afford to take any chances.

My nerves were more than a tad on edge when I got on my stepladder and began screwing the showerhead back into place—afraid that any minute Norman Bates, dressed as his dead mother, would come storming in and stab me to death.

What can I say? I've got a highly active imagination.

And my near death-by-showerhead wasn't the only thing haunting me. I shuddered to think what goofy plan Daddy had up his sleeve to give his Statue of Liberty the "exposure" it deserved.

Most upsetting of all, I kept replaying my disastrous

visit to Hapi House last night, killing Cleopatra, Hapi's holy beetle—and the frosty way Dickie had kissed me good-bye.

I checked my phone, hoping Dickie had texted me.

Nada.

So I texted him a perky, Morning there, you! Thanks so much for the creative energy crystal! XOXO

No reply.

"Oh, Pro." I sighed. "I think I screwed things up with Dickie."

My precious princess looked up from where she was belching minced mackerel fumes.

Congratulations! You go, girl!

All of which is why I was in a bit of funk as I headed off to La Belle Vie that morning, my creative energy crystal nestled in my purse along with the *Hapi Way of Life* pamphlet.

After parking my Corolla in Daisy's driveway, I hustled to the kitchen for a cup of coffee. There I found Raymond and Solange wrapped in a steamy embrace, the kind of embrace I'd been hoping to get from Dickie last night.

They sprang apart at the sight of me, grinning from ear to ear.

"Hey, guys," I said. "How's it going? Silly question. I can see things are going great with you two."

"Couldn't be happier," Raymond beamed.

"What about Daisy? How's she doing?"

"Still grieving," Solange said. "But Esme's convinced her to go out for a spa day. I'm sure it will do her a world of good."

And a free spa treatment on Daisy's dime wouldn't hurt Esme either, I thought, most uncharitably.

Back in my office, I settled down at my desk, where for the fourth time that morning (okay, the thirteenth time), I checked for a text from Dickie.

Still nothing.

With a sigh, I reached into my purse for the creative energy crystal he'd given me and put it alongside my computer, hoping it would act like a router and stream fabulous ideas into my laptop without any heavy lifting from *moi*.

Then I fished out the Hapi-ness pamphlet and, fortified by a healthy swig of coffee, began to read it. It was every bit as gloppy as I feared it would be, a cliché-ridden ode to the Hapi Way of Life, the joys of meditation and vegan diets, the power of affirmations, and the evils of red meat.

I was struggling to stay awake when I saw something that grabbed my attention. Along with the dratted beetle, it turned out that the lotus plant was also high up on Hapi's Holy List.

And just like that, I'd found a way to make amends for last night's Cleopatra disaster. I'd buy Hapi a lotus plant!

I'd hand-deliver it to Hapi House, and filled with gratitude, Hapi would forgive me for squishing poor Cleopatra. With any luck, he'd share my thoughtful gesture with Dickie, who, in turn, would wrap me in his manly arms for a smooch.

Yes, time to get started on Operation Lotus Plant.

Which wasn't quite as easy as I thought. Lotus plants are not exactly a hot seller in most nurseries. But at last I located one at Hashimoto Garden Supplies in West Los Angeles.

They had one for sale for a whopping fifty bucks.

Hang the expense. It'd be worth it.

In a flash, I grabbed my purse and was tooling over to the nursery—glad that Daisy was off at the spa and not there to see me running out on C. Weatherly.

A half hour later, I walked out of Hashimoto's, fifty dollars poorer, a beautiful pink lotus plant nestled in my arms.

It took me ages to slog my way over to Hollywood, but I remained relentlessly perky, shrugging off road closures and drivers darting out from nowhere at Indy 500 speeds only to slow down to a crawl once they'd landed in front of me.

Yes, indeedie, I was a hopeful camper when I pulled into a parking spot a mere six blocks from Hapi House, confident my beautiful lotus plant would mend any broken fences with Hapi, and—by extension—Dickie. Sheltering the precious bloom in my arms, I fairly skipped those six blocks to Hapi House.

In broad daylight, the bungalow was even more run-down than it had looked last night. I rang the bell, and seconds later Hapi came to the door, no longer in a flowing robe but in jeans and a Three Stooges T-shirt.

I have to admit I was surprised by his outfit. Not exactly guru garb.

"Oh, it's you," he said, giving me the stink eye.

And then I caught a whiff of something in the air. Was it my imagination, or did I smell meat cooking? No, it couldn't be. Hapi was a strict vegetarian. It must have been coming from next door.

"I feel so bad about what happened to poor Cleopatra," I said, launching into my prepared speech, "I got you this holy lotus plant, hoping it will ease your pain."

"Yeah, okay." He grabbed it from me, barely glancing at it, clearly eager to get rid of me.

And then I heard a woman's voice calling:

"Hey, Marty. You want mustard or ketchup with your burger?"

Burger?? I took another sniff. This time, there was no doubt about it. I smelled meat cooking—not next door, but here in Hapi House.

Whaddaya know? Dickie's holier-than-thou guru was a carnivorous Three Stooges fan!

Gotcha! I felt like crying out.

Instead, I opted for a simpering smile and a cheery, "Enjoy your burger, Marty!"

He had the good grace to blush before slamming the door in my face.

Chapter 31

So Hapi was a fake.

My first instinct was to call Dickie and break the news to him. Hopefully, he'd be so disillusioned he'd give up his god-awful vegan diet. And I wouldn't have to suffer through any more kale and tofu salads.

But maybe that wasn't such a smart idea. Dickie might not believe me and be angry with me for casting aspersions on his beloved guru. No, best to keep my mouth shut for the time being.

In the meanwhile, the smell of Hapi/Marty's burger had me hankering for a nice juicy Quarter Pounder. As I drove back to Daisy's, I kept my eyes peeled for a Mickey D's. Usually they're everywhere. But now, when I was dying for a burger, there wasn't a golden arch in sight.

I was driving along on my burger prowl when I noticed a sign for a restaurant called Christophe.

Wait a minute. Wasn't that the fancy French restaurant where Raymond had been a chef? I doubted they'd serve burgers, but I decided to stop in anyway. I hadn't forgotten about Raymond's phony alibi for the day of the murder, and I wanted to see what dirt I could dig up on him.

Unwilling to spend one more minute scouring the streets for a parking spot, I forked over eight bucks to have a valet park my Corolla. Heaven knows where he was going to find a space for it. Probably somewhere in Burbank.

After watching him lurch off in my car, I made my way into the restaurant, a minimalist joint where everything was white: the walls, the tablecloths, the chairs, the customers.

The only spot of color was the deep eggplant carpeting.

A few diners were scattered around the room, impeccably dressed and reeking of money. Needless to say, I was way out of place in my elastic waist jeans and L.L.Bean crew neck.

A pencil-thin maître d' stood behind a podium, eyeing me much as he'd look at a cockroach who'd just strolled in off the street.

"Reservations?" he asked.

"Plenty. But I'm eating here anyway."

Of course I didn't really say that, but merely confessed I'd not booked a table in advance.

He pursed his lips in disapproval and with a reluctant sigh led me to a distant table near the kitchen, clearly the gulag of the restaurant.

"*Bon appétit*," he muttered, still eyeing me askance as he tossed me a leather-bound menu.

I opened it and gasped in disbelief.

I thought the valet was expensive. The menu made the parking look like a Bluelight Special at Kmart.

The prices started at fifteen bucks and skyrocketed up to the nineties.

What's worse, everything was written in French.

I was still reeling from the prices when two busboys descended on me: One brought me a glass of water, while the other lifted a warm roll from a basket with a pair of tongs and gently set it down on my butter plate.

I sure hoped the roll was free. If so, I wondered if I could get away with eating bread and water for lunch.

It was then that I was approached by my wannabe actress/waitress, a stunning young blonde straight out of a Hitchcock movie, Grace Kelly reincarnated. Unlike the surly maître d', she flashed me a welcoming smile and asked if she could get me anything to drink. Some wine, perhaps?

I assured her that water was just fine.

"Have you decided what you'd like to eat?" G. Kelly asked.

"Yes, I'll have this," I said, pointing to something I'd discovered at the bottom of the menu for only six bucks. Whatever it was, I was ordering it.

"I'm sorry," she said, "but that's the service charge for splitting an entrée."

Talk about mortified. Thanks heavens Mrs. Wallis, my high school French teacher, wasn't there to witness my humiliation.

I guess G. Kelly saw how embarrassed I was, because

she then leaned in and whispered conspiratorially, "The prices here are ridiculous."

What a sweet, understanding young woman! I only hoped she'd win an Oscar one day.

"How about this?" I asked, pointing to one of the fifteen-dollar appetizers.

"Octopus in a baby corn and artichoke coulis," she said, shaking her head in warning. "Not one of my favorites."

"You pick something for me."

Hopefully something I wouldn't need to take out a bank loan to pay for.

"You like pasta?" she asked.

"Love it," I said.

After pizza it's my favorite P food, with peanut butter a close third.

"Get the tagliatelle and mushroom appetizer," she said, pointing to one of the fifteen-dollar dishes. "It's one of the few items on the menu that isn't French and it's really good."

I thanked her for her recommendation, and she floated off to place my order.

By now I was fairly peckish and scarfed down my roll in record time. I was salivating at the thought of a heaping plate of pasta when G. Kelly returned with my tagliatelle.

She placed it in front of me and I blinked in disbelief.

There, in the middle of the plate, was a tiny mound of pasta about the size of a potato pancake.

Never had I seen such a small portion.

"Believe it or not," G. Kelly said, seeing the look of astonishment on my face, "this is one of our more generous appetizers."

Holy moly. No wonder the rich were so thin!

I inhaled it in about three bites, and seconds later a busboy was whisking away my plate.

Soon after that, G. Kelly returned.

"Any room for dessert?" she asked.

Was she kidding? That tagliatelle was rattling around my tummy like a pinball in outer space.

"Nope. I'm stuffed."

We both had a hearty chuckle over that one.

I'd been so gobsmacked by Christophe's nosebleed-expensive prices, I'd almost forgotten the reason I stopped by. Time to get some dirt on Raymond.

Luckily the place was still pretty empty, so G. Kelly had time to gab.

"I suppose you're wondering what I'm doing here," I said when she brought me my check.

"I figured you were a tourist who didn't know any better."

"Actually, I know someone who used to work here. A chef named Raymond."

"Really?" she asked, taken aback. "Raymond is a friend of yours?"

"More of an acquaintance. He's a private chef for the woman I work for."

"Wow," G. Kelly said, shaking her head in wonder. "He's still working as a chef? After what happened here, I didn't think he'd be able to land a job anywhere."

I perked up, interested. I sensed some hot gossip coming down the pike.

"Why?" I asked. "What happened?"

She looked around to make sure no one was watching and leaned in to tell me.

"He got into a big fight with Christophe, went running after him with a butcher's knife. Fortunately the dish-washers were able to restrain him. Christophe fired him on the spot. It was all over the restaurant grapevine. I thought he'd never work again.

"Whoops," she said, "some poor suckers just sat at one of my tables. Gotta run."

She dashed off, and I paid the bill, leaving her a very generous tip—for excellent service and the fascinating nugget of info she'd just lobbed in my lap.

So Raymond had a history of violence, attacking his employer. With a knife, yet.

Who knows? Maybe he'd gone after Tommy, too.

Only this time, maybe he got the job done.

Chapter 32

I finally found a Mickey D's, where I proceeded to scarf down a Quarter Pounder in record time. I figured I didn't need any fries, what with the roll and tagliatelle I'd eaten at Christophe. But I ordered them anyway.

Sue me.

Driving back to Daisy's, I intended to corner Raymond in the kitchen and confront him with what I'd discovered. But before I even had a chance to put my purse in my desk drawer, he came storming into my office.

"I got a call from my brother a little while ago," he said, oozing fury.

I recoiled in horror. Not because he'd spoken with his brother, but because in his hand he held a large, gleaming butcher's knife.

Omigod. The man was a homicidal maniac! Was history about to repeat itself? Was I about to be sliced and diced to oblivion?

"Take one step closer with that knife," I said, my voice a terrified squeak, "and I'll scream."

He looked down at the knife, as if puzzled to find it there.

"Don't be an idiot," he said, putting it down on Kate's desk. "I was trimming a rack of lamb when I heard you come in, and I was so damn mad I forgot I had it in my hand."

My heart, which had been thumping like a conga drum, resumed its normal beat.

Raymond, on the other hand, was still red-faced with anger, somewhere between a simmer and a high boil.

"My brother told me someone passing herself off as 'Detective Mildred Pierce' stopped by his house to question him. It turns out she wasn't a cop after all, which he found out when the real police stopped by in the middle of her visit. And according to my brother's description of Detective Pierce, she looked an awful lot like you."

"Guilty as charged," I confessed.

"What the hell were you doing there?"

By now he was definitely at full boil. But seeing as he had abandoned his knife, I wasn't about to be intimidated.

"I was busting your alibi for the morning of the murder. Before the real cops showed up, I had quite an informative chat with your brother. Apparently while you were shopping for a coffee table at Home Depot, your brother was looking for a coffeemaker at Ikea."

And just like that, the stuffing was knocked out of him.

"I knew I shouldn't have trusted that idiot to stick with the script," Raymond sighed, slumping down in Kate's chair.

"And it gets worse. I just had lunch at a charming little restaurant called Christophe, where I was served the smallest meal in the history of dining—along with an interesting tale about you chasing Christophe with a butcher's knife."

"Okay," he groaned, "I wasn't with my brother the morning of the murder. I was out interviewing for another job. I knew it wasn't going to be easy landing one given what happened with Christophe. But I couldn't stand Tommy bossing me around one more minute. And the last thing I want is for Daisy to find out, especially now that she's raised our salaries back to where they were before Tommy slashed them. So, yes, I've been lying about my alibi, but I swear I didn't kill Tommy."

Maybe he did. Maybe he didn't.

All I knew was that I intended to keep a safe distance between me and his butcher's knife.

Chapter 33

I don't know how much more of this I can stand,
Clarissa thought.

The sun beat down on her back as she wielded
her pickax, digging turquoise nuggets from the
rocky shoals.

But it wasn't the sun that was stoking her fire.
No, it was her proximity to Max Laredo, the gruff
turquoise miner who, after several weeks by her
side, no longer seemed quite so gruff.

Now she turned to see that he'd taken off his
T-shirt, and before she could stop herself, she
gasped at the sight of his bronzed muscles and six-
pack abs glistening in the blazing sun.

"Ms. Weatherly? Are you all right?"

Max was looking at her with eyes as blue as the
turquoise they were mining.

"I . . . I'm fine," Clarissa managed to say, trying not to stare at those magnificent abs.

"Well, I'm not," Max said, taking their pickaxes and flinging them aside. "I've been wanting to do this ever since I first laid eyes on you!"

And with that he wrapped her in his sinewy arms, where they clung together, lips locked, sweat mingling, two hearts beating as one.

Clarissa was groaning in ecstasy at the feel of Max's rugged body next to hers when suddenly she heard her cell phone ringing—and ringing—and ringing—

No, wait. That wasn't Clarissa's phone. It was mine.

It was the day after my confrontation with Raymond and his butcher's knife, and I'd been at my desk all morning, churning out torrid prose for C. Weatherly. Now I clicked open my phone and did a little gasping of my own to see a text from Dickie!

Sorry I've been AWOL. Swamped at work. Dinner at my condo this Saturday?

And just like that, Disney bluebirds were chirping on my shoulder.

I hadn't messed things up with Dickie, after all!

Wasting no time, I typed in an enthusiastic You betcha!

It was hard to concentrate on C. Weatherly after that. The only steamy love scenes I seemed to dream up were ones involving me, Dickie, and a vat of Chunky Monkey.

I was utterly lost in fantasyland until noon, when Solange poked her head in the door.

"Lunch on the patio," she announced. "Lobster salad."

Lobster salad, huh? At last, something to yank me back to reality.

Out on the patio, Daisy sat bracketed by Clayton and Esme—Clayton firmly ensconced in "Tommy's" chair, boasting about a tennis match he'd just played.

"And then I beat him, 40–love. It was an absolute triumph!"

Across from Clayton, Esme sat, tall and regal, a cruise brochure splayed out in front of her.

"Jaine, dear," Daisy said, catching sight of me. "Come join us."

She was clad in her usual turquoise, but I couldn't help but notice the dark circles under her eyes. I suspected she wasn't getting very much sleep.

"How's the book coming along?" she asked, as I took a seat next to Esme.

"Great!"

"I don't have the energy to read it right now," she said with a wan smile. "But I will soon. I promise."

"Daisy, darling," Esme clucked. "You're exhausted. I can't wait till we set sail on our cruise. It's just what you need to restore your spirits."

"I'm so happy you were able to get tickets to join us," Daisy said to Clayton.

"Wouldn't miss it for the world!" he said, patting her hand.

"And don't forget the Bel Air Animal Welfare League luncheon next week," Esme said. "That should be so much fun!"

No doubt about it. Clayton and Esme were back in the saddle, having resumed their former roles as Daisy's besties.

And they weren't the only ones in a good mood.

Solange had a definite spring in her step as she moved around the table, serving us our lobster salads.

Which were, to quote Esme, "Divine! Simply Divine!"

At the end of the meal, Daisy summoned Raymond from the kitchen to tell him what a wonderful job he'd done.

"My pleasure, Ms. Kincaid," beamed the ponytailed chef.

I watched Daisy as she graced everyone with her wan smile.

The poor woman didn't have a clue that one of them was a killer.

Chapter 34

As it turned out, there was another hot suspect waiting in the wings.

I was at Kate's computer later that afternoon paying Daisy's bills when I came across a check made out to Arlene Zimmer—Tommy's Wonder Woman ex-girlfriend.

I remembered how furious she'd been the day she stormed into the living room at La Belle Vie, going postal on Tommy, trying to strangle him. Up to this point, I hadn't considered her a suspect because she wasn't at the house the day of the murder. But now I wondered if she'd found a way to sneak into La Belle Vie and knock off her cheating ex.

Thanks to the helpful folks at whitepages.com, I got what I hoped was Arlene's address and left work early to track her down.

Following Google Maps' prompts, I wound up at a modern high-rise in Hollywood, with a NOW LEASING! banner strung across the front apartments. In a rare burst of good luck, I found a place to park in front of the building, and soon I was at the intercom, buzzing Arlene Zimmer's apartment.

No answer. Damn! I should've called first.

I returned to my car and was merging back into traffic when I saw a bright red Miata zooming out of the building's underground parking. The vanity plates on the car read ARLENEZ. It had to be her.

It looked like lady luck was back at my side.

Soon I was following ARLENEZ along Santa Monica Boulevard, going farther and farther east, the buildings growing shabbier with each block, until she pulled into the parking lot of a place called The Body Shop. A billboard of a pouty blonde with unnaturally ginormous boobs atop the building let me know this was not an auto repair establishment.

If I wasn't mistaken, it looked like Arlene Zimmer was a stripper.

I pulled in after her and watched her emerge from her Miata in a belted trench coat and backbreaking five-inch stilettos. Her battleship boobs were poised for action, makeup slathered on with a trowel, hair puffed out with enough extensions to upholster a small sofa.

It was Tommy's ex-girlfriend, all right. I bolted out of my car and sprinted after her as she headed for a side entrance.

"Wait up!" I called out. "I need to talk to you."

Either she didn't hear me or she wasn't in the mood for a chat. Before I could catch up with her, she'd disappeared into the building.

I was about to follow her when I heard a booming voice:

"Where do you think you're going?"

I turned to see a hulking bulldog of a man glowering down at me.

"I need to speak to the woman who just went inside."

"Sorry," he said, planting his hammy fist on the door. "Our entertainers speak only to paying customers."

Accent on the *paying*.

"The only way you're getting into the club is through the front door," he said, leading me to The Body Shop's main entrance and waving me inside to a dank hallway.

There I was greeted by another goon perched on a stool, who expected me to fork over thirty bucks for a cover charge.

"Thirty dollars?" I balked.

"You don't get to look for free, sweetie. This ain't a charity."

Reluctantly I handed him my credit card, hoping the gang at Visa wouldn't judge me too harshly when they saw the charge on my bill.

Once inside the club—a dimly lit room reeking of beer and Mr. Clean—a bored, gum-chewing gal in a threadbare bikini ushered me to a table at the front of the house.

At this hour, the place was pretty empty except for a few glassy-eyed lechers and a bunch of rowdy college kids. The college kids, in USC sweatshirts, testosterone run amok, were shouting crude comments at the topless dancers—way too crude for your delicate ears.

Let's just say they wanted to give great big hugs to the nice ladies onstage.

One of whom was Arlene Zimmer, listlessly shaking her stuff in a G-string and pasties. Seated so close to the stage, I could hear her saying to the gal next to her, "I hate working this shift. Just a bunch of losers and lesbos."

That last zinger directed at *moi*.

Before I could call her out on her politically incorrect term of address, I was approached by the same gum-chewing honey who'd led me to my seat.

"So what'll it be?" she asked.

"Diet Coke."

"We got a three-drink minimum. Cokes are twelve bucks apiece."

Yikes. It was expensive being a sexist pig.

I told her to bring on the Cokes and turned my attention back to the stage, where Arlene was now within whispering distance.

"Excuse me, Arlene," I said.

She looked down at me, peeved.

"My name isn't Arlene in here. It's Misty. Misty Harbor."

"Sorry, Ms. Harbor. We met a while back at Daisy Kincaid's home."

She squinted at me through a thick fringe of false eyelashes.

"Oh, yeah. You were the one stuffing your face with a Ding Dong."

I decided to take the high road and let that crack slide.

"I was wondering if I could talk to you after the show about Tommy LaSalle's murder."

A calculating look flashed in her eyes.

"That depends. You wanna talk, you gotta tip."

She thrust out her G-string, where some of the degenerates in the audience had already planted dollar bills.

I grabbed a dollar from my wallet and gingerly hung it from her hip.

"Go for it, Cocoa Puffs!" one of the college idiots called out as I gave her the money.

(Note to self: CUCKOO FOR COCOA PUFFS T-shirt inappropriate attire for strip clubs.)

"A buck?" Arlene snorted in disgust. "For that kinda money, all you're getting is 'No comment.'"

Reluctantly I parted with a twenty.

Ca-ching.

"Meet you in the parking lot on my break," she said.

"Take it off! Take it off!" the USC scholars were now chanting at the dancers.

When I got up to go, one of them shouted at me, "Put it on!"

Which got a hearty round of guffaws from his buddies.

I hoped the little twerp got mono.

"Buzz off, bozo!" I sputtered. "Go back to school and read a book! I'm thoroughly disgusted by the objectification and denigration of women in this dive, not to mention the absurd three-drink minimum and thirty-dollar cover charge. I will be writing a letter to Gloria Steinem to protest this sorrowful state of affairs. In the meanwhile, I urge you clowns to grow up and get a life."

Actually, that's what I intended to say. Alas, I didn't get past, "Buzz off, bozo!" when the two goons I'd seen earlier magically appeared at my side, lifting me up and whisking me out of the room.

"Wait!" I protested. "I'm not finished."

"Yes, you are," one of the goons said as they shoved me out into the parking lot.

"Bye-bye, Cocoa Puffs," said the other, with a most irritating snicker.

*   *   *

I waited in my Corolla for what seemed like ages until Arlene finally emerged from The Body Shop in her trench coat, tottering toward me on her mile-high stilettos.

"My dogs are killing me!" she said, kicking off her shoes as she settled into the passenger seat, her battleship boobs practically grazing the dashboard.

Then she took a jar of Mineral Ice from the pocket of her trench coat and began rubbing a glob of the blue goo onto her instep.

"So what are you, anyway? Some kind of private eye?"

"Part-time, semi-professional. A friend of mine is a suspect in the case, and I'm trying to clear her name."

"I'm afraid you're wasting your time," she said, rubbing the blue goo on her other foot.

By now the Corolla smelled like a eucalyptus grove.

"I don't know a thing about Tommy's murder. All I know is he's dead. And I can't say I'm surprised. The guy screwed over so many people, it was bound to catch up with him sooner or later."

"Any idea who might have killed him?"

"Not a clue," she shrugged. "Well, if that's all," she added, putting the lid back on her Mineral Ice, "I've got to get back to the pervs."

But I couldn't let her go. Not yet. Time to spring my little trap.

"One more thing. I happen to have a witness who saw you leaving La Belle Vie at the time of the murder."

A monumental whopper, but she didn't know that.

"That's a lie!" she said, eyes blazing. "I was out of the house by six AM that morning."

Bingo! My trap door had just slammed shut.

She clamped her hand over her mouth, realizing what a boo boo she'd just made.

"So you were at La Belle Vie the day of the murder?"

"Yeah, I was there," she confessed. "After the old lady paid me off, Tommy came down to the club and sweet-talked his way back into my life. He swore he didn't love Daisy, that he planned to marry her and cash out big time in a divorce. After that, he promised, we'd be together for good. And like the patsy I am, I fell for it. He gave me a key to the mansion, along with the alarm code, and soon I was sneaking over in the middle of the night. But I swear I'm not the one who bumped him off. I was out of the house that morning by six."

She sounded sincere, but I wasn't quite convinced.

Once again, I remembered how furious she'd been the day she'd stormed into La Belle Vie, going straight for Tommy's jugular. Maybe that last night with Tommy she'd found out he'd been making the moves on Solange—or one of the many other women he'd probably been pursuing. After all, he'd even come on to me.

Maybe she'd been humiliated one time too often and—armed with the key he'd given her—had returned to La Belle Vie to put an end to Tommy's cheating ways forever.

Chapter 35

A nasty surprise was waiting for me when I got home from The Body Shop.

The minute I walked in the door, I saw the place had been trashed—books knocked down from my bookshelf, philodendron overturned, sofa cushions upended. In the kitchen, the garbage can was on its side, the floor littered with old pizza crusts.

A bolt of fear shot through me.

The killer had returned! The showerhead incident was no accident. It was the killer who'd loosened it. And whoever it was had come back to put another scare in me.

But, wait. That couldn't be. I'd had my locks changed. And there was no key under the flowerpot anymore. What's more, when I checked my windows, I found no signs of forced entry.

Then it hit me. I knew who the culprit was: my fractious furball, who was lounging on my armchair, a piece of philodendron leaf lodged in her fur.

"You did this, didn't you, Pro?"

She gazed up at me through slitted eyes.

I refuse to answer on the grounds that it may incriminate me.

"This is about Dickie, isn't it? You're not going to be happy until he's out of my life. Well, I've got news for you, young lady. I'm not about to give him up. You can make all the mess you want, but I'm not going to change my mind! I will not be dictated to by my cat!"

Strong words, but alas, they had little impact.

All I got from her was a cavernous yawn.

Yeah, right. Whatever. When you're through cleaning up, I'd like a snack.

I spent the next hour or so cursing like a sailor while I put my apartment back in order.

I'd just swept the last of the garbage back into the trash can when Lance came knocking at my door.

"You're not going to believe what happened!" he said, rushing in and plopping down on my sofa. "I had dinner with a certified Looney Tunes Internet date at an all-you-can-eat Chinese buffet. Not only did the guy pick every single piece of shrimp from the tray of shrimp lo mein, but before we left, he filled three plastic containers with wonton soup to go!"

"You poor thing," I said, wrapping a sympathetic arm around his shoulder. "That really is unbelievable."

"No, no. That's not the unbelievable part. I have to tell you what happened when I was driving home. I passed Porta Via, that fancy restaurant in Beverly Hills, and you'll never guess who I saw parking cars!"

"Who?"

"Dickie! The guy works as a valet parker!"

I whipped back my arm from his shoulder, furious.

"You really don't know how to be happy for me, do you? You're just like Prozac. You'd do anything to break up me and Dickie."

"That's not true! I could swear it was Dickie parking that car."

"Really? Dickie is a valet parker? The man who drives a BMW and lives in a condo with a view of the Pacific? I don't think so."

By now I was seething.

Lance had pulled a lot of annoying stunts during the course of our friendship, but this time he'd gone too far.

"I think you'd better leave," I said, holding open the door. "Until you can be happy for me, I'm not sure we can still be friends."

"Please, Jaine. Don't do this."

He shot me a sad, doe-eyed look, much like Prozac on the rare occasions she's trying to make amends.

But it wasn't going to work.

"Just go."

He walked down the path to his apartment, blond curls wilted, shoulders slumped.

Thoroughly aggravated, I headed for the tub with my reliable buddy, Mr. Chardonnay. I tried to relax, but I couldn't. I was too upset.

Later I was lying in bed, staring up at the ceiling, Prozac belching hearty halibut fumes at my side, when I heard Lance tapping on the paper-thin wall between us.

"Jaine, are you asleep?"

"Yes. Leave me alone."

"I'm so sorry, honey. I didn't mean to upset you. Please forgive me. Maybe it wasn't Dickie I saw parking that car. Maybe it was somebody else."

He sounded so miserable, I melted.

"That's okay, Lance. Forget it."

"So we're good?"

"We're good."

But deep in my heart, I wasn't so sure we were.

Chapter 36

"Any news?"

I sat at my desk at La Belle Vie and groaned. It was Kate, calling for a progress report. Or, in my case, lack of progress report.

"I've got a few more leads," I said, "but still no solid evidence."

"Why don't you come to my place for dinner so we can talk? I'm going stir crazy here without a job."

"Great. But let me buy dinner." The last thing Kate needed was to spend money on me now that she was unemployed. "How about I pick up something from KFC?"

"That would be wonderful!"

And so at seven that night I was tooling over to Kate's apartment in Mar Vista, armed with a bucket of the Colonel's chicken, biscuits, coleslaw, and mashed potatoes.

Not to mention a bottle of Trader Joe's finest bargain chardonnay.

Kate lived in a modest section of Mar Vista, several blocks away from the crest of land that actually offered a vista of the sea. But it was a pretty street, lined with jacaranda trees and 1970s-era apartments.

I parked in front of Kate's place—Vista Gardens—a three-story stucco building with patio units on the first floor. Heading up to the entrance, I saw several people out on one of the patios enjoying wine and cheese.

After Kate buzzed me in, I took the elevator to her apartment on the second floor, where she greeted me in shabby sweats, her curly hair gone wild in Mad Scientist mode. Like Daisy, she had bags under her eyes the size of carry-ons.

"Jaine!" she cried. "I'm so happy you came. And look at all the goodies you brought! Let's set them down on the coffee table. I thought we could eat in the living room. The dining room's so cramped."

She led me past a tiny kitchen/dining area and into her living room, the coffee table already set with plates, silverware, and wine glasses.

Although her apartment was small, it was tastefully decorated—very West Coast Hamptons, with lots of white wicker, pine, and coordinating stripes and florals.

"What a cute place," I said, looking around.

"I only hope I can afford to stay here," Kate sighed. "I'm already behind on my rent."

Once again, I felt a stab of guilt for having made so little progress tracking down Tommy's killer.

"Thanks so much for bringing the chicken!"

"I got Extra-Crispy."

"Just the way I like it," she said. "Want to relax first with a glass of wine, or should we dig right in?"

"How about we dig right in with a glass of wine?"

"A girl after my own heart," she grinned, opening the screw top on my Chateau Joe.

Ensconced on her white wicker sofa, we chowed down on our chicken with gusto. For a while, the only sounds in the room were those of fingers being licked.

Finally, I managed to tear myself away from a chicken thigh long enough to give Kate an update on my investigation. I told her how Tommy had been blackmailing Solange into having sex with him, and how he'd slashed Daisy's contributions to Esme's fake charity. How Clayton had lied about being out of town on the day of the murder. About Raymond's history of violence at Christophe. And finally, about Arlene Zimmer's handy dandy key to La Belle Vie.

"So there you have it," I said, reaching for a biscuit. "Plenty of suspects, but no viable evidence linking any of them to the crime."

"My money's on Esme. She's the one who threw me under the bus, telling the cops she'd seen me going to the gym."

"You could be right. With Tommy out of the picture, Daisy's funding Esme's charity again, and the two of them are heading off on a Tahitian cruise with Clayton."

"It's ironic, isn't it?" Kate said. "I'm the cops' number one suspect, and yet I'm the only person who's miserable now that Tommy's gone."

We were sitting there musing on this unhappy state of affairs when we heard a blast of rock music coming from the patio below. Probably the wine-and-cheese gang I'd seen earlier.

Without missing a beat, Kate leaped up and raced to her front window, yanking it open.

"Turn down your stereo!" she hollered at the top of her lungs. "Damn neighbors are impossible!" she grunted, stomping back to the sofa.

A few seconds later, the music was muted. But this wasn't enough for Kate. Chicken wing in hand, she stormed back to the window.

"I can still hear it, you idiots!"

I must confess I was more than a tad taken aback. She'd asked the people downstairs to turn down their music, and they did. Why was she so angry?

Now they turned it down even more, so that it was barely audible.

When she came back to the sofa, I tried to engage her in conversation, telling her about my miniscule meal at Christophe. But I could see she wasn't listening, grinding her teeth at every faint beat of the music below.

"I practically needed a GPS system to find the food on my plate," I was saying when she exploded:

"One of these days, I'm going to take a hammer and smash that stereo to smithereens!"

With that, she jumped up and grabbed her plate of chicken bones.

"Let's see how well *these* go with their music."

"What're you doing?" I asked, wide-eyed.

"I'm going to throw my chicken bones on their stupid party. Yours, too," she said, grabbing my plate.

She started for the window with the plates in her hands.

"Kate, you can't go dumping chicken bones on somebody's patio!" I said, racing to her side and whisking the plates away from her. "We can barely hear the music. And besides, what if they call the police? That's the last thing you need."

"Oh, God, you're right."

Just as quickly as it had appeared, the anger drained from her face, Dr. Jekyll turning back to Mr. Hyde. (Or the other way around; I can never remember who the crazy one is.)

"Excuse the outburst." She sank back down on the sofa. "I know I overreacted. I've been off my meds for a while."

"Meds?" I asked, putting the chicken bones on her kitchen counter, safely out of reach.

"Antidepressants. They calm me down, but I hate the damn things. They give me raging insomnia."

"That's too bad. When did you stop taking them?"

"I'm not sure. I think it was a couple of days before Tommy got killed."

Suddenly a sick feeling began roiling around my stomach along with all that extra crispy chicken.

This woman with major anger management issues had gone off her meds right before Tommy's murder. Which meant she could have been perfectly capable of marching over to the gym and knifing him to death.

Had I been wrong all along? Had Kate conned me into investigating Tommy's murder—not to clear her name, but to cast suspicion on somebody else?

I tried to act as if everything was fine as I helped her do the dishes and plowed through a pint of fudge ripple for dessert. But all the camaraderie I'd felt for her had vanished, replaced by a wellspring of doubt.

"I guess I'd better get going," I said, once the dishes were done, eager to vamoose.

"But you can't go yet. You haven't seen my collection!"

"Collection? Of what?"

"C'mon, I'll show you."

She took me by the hand and led me to her bedroom, done up in the same beachy motif as her living room. With one jarring exception: a wooden étagère crammed with voodoo dolls—all riddled with pins.

And perched among them was an alarming little opus called *Hexes for All Occasions: How to Cast Spells for Vengeance and Harm.*

Holy mackerel. I thought Voodoo Tommy was just a joke. But it looked like Kate took this stuff seriously.

"My enemies list," she said, gesturing to the dolls. "Meet everyone who's ever pissed me off. I've got a whole shelf devoted to my downstairs neighbors. So far, my hexes haven't worked. But I keep trying."

Talk about misreading someone! Underneath her mop of curls and elastic waist pants, Kate was seriously wackadoodle.

By now I couldn't wait to get out of her apartment.

"I've really got to run," I said.

"Can't you stay a bit longer?"

"Sorry, but I've got a ton of work to do on Daisy's book."

"Well, okay," she said grudgingly, "but I'm counting on you to get me out of this mess. Don't let me down, or you'll wind up on my voodoo shelf. Haha."

I forced a weak laugh but wasted no time grabbing my purse and sprinting out the door.

"Let's do this again soon," Kate called after me.

"Absolutely," I lied.

She stood in the hallway watching me as I hurried to the elevator, which took forever to show up. Finally the doors opened, and I practically leaped in.

Minutes later, I was speeding back home in my Corolla, wondering if I'd just chowed down on extra-crispy chicken with Tommy's killer.

YOU'VE GOT MAIL!

TAMPA VISTAS GAZETTE

MAYHEM AT THE MICHELANGELO GALLERY

The Grand Unveiling of Lydia Pinkus's much-acclaimed torso of Sir Isaac Newton at the Michelangelo Art Gallery was disrupted last night when one of the guests accidentally sent the sculpture toppling to the ground.

"Although I'm not so sure it was an accident," a clearly peeved Ms. Pinkus opined.

The event was also marred by what several attendees described as a "god-awful fishy smell."

To: Jausten
From: Shoptillyoudrop
Subject: Daddy Does It Again!

I knew Lydia's unveiling ceremony was going to be a disaster the minute we pulled into the parking lot and Daddy took out his gummy bear with a torch—I mean, Statue of Liberty—from where he'd hidden it in the trunk of the Camry.

"Hank Austen!" I said. "You can't possibly bring that thing into the gallery."

"And deny the art lovers of Tampa the chance to see it? Never!"

Then in he marched to the gallery, bold as brass, his silly Statue of Liberty in the crook of one arm, the other arm free to scarf down hors d'oeuvres from the buffet.

Needless to say, I stayed as far away from him as possible, hiding in a corner behind a statue of a naked lady.

Peeking over the naked lady's shoulder, I saw Lydia in the center of the room, surrounded by a sea of well-wishers. Next to her was her torso of Sir Isaac Newton, perched on a pedestal and covered with a black cloth, to be whipped away at the Grand Unveiling.

Way too embarrassed to face her, I stayed huddled in the corner.

Darling Edna Lindstrom saw me hiding and hurried over with some franks in a blanket, which I was way too upset to eat. (Okay, I ate them, but they tasted like chalk in my mouth.)

Edna assured me that everyone was used to Daddy's crazy antics by now and begged me to come out of hiding, but I couldn't bear to show my face.

I was huddled behind the statue of the naked lady when an artsy-looking woman in a bright red beret wandered over to my side, puffing on an e-cigarette.

"Who is that foul-smelling man," she said, waving her e-cigarette at Daddy, "holding the statue of a gummy bear?"

"I have no idea," I said with a feeble smile, and breathed a sigh of relief when she wandered away.

At last the big moment arrived. Time for the Grand Unveiling. Molly, our instructor, stood beside Lydia and clinked her champagne glass to get everyone's attention. After welcoming us all to her gallery, she went on to talk about what an amazing sculptor Lydia was, calling her "the most talented student I've had in all my years of teaching.

"Without any further ado," she then said, "the Michelangelo Gallery is proud to present Sir Isaac Newton by Lydia Pinkus!"

With that, she whipped off the cloth covering the statue and everyone burst into applause at the sight of Sir Isaac.

(Everyone except for Daddy, who was pouting in a most unsportsmanlike manner.)

Then suddenly, amidst all the oohs and aahs, a flying ball of fur came zooming across the room, making a

beeline for Daddy, who was standing with his Statue of
Liberty in one hand and a cheese puff in the other.

"Michelangelo!" Molly cried.

It turned out Molly's cat, Michelangelo, had escaped
from Molly's office where he'd been stowed away,
lured by the smell of Daddy's fishy hair. He reminded
me so much of your darling Zoloft as he leaped through
the air and landed on Daddy's shoulder.

Daddy, caught by surprise, stumbled backward toward
Lydia's torso, his arms flailing about wildly as he tried to
keep his balance.

But it was no use. We all gasped as he went slamming
into Sir Isaac Newton and sent it toppling to the floor.

"His nose!" Lydia cried. "Sir Isaac Newton's nose broke
off!"

Sure enough, poor Sir Isaac had lost his nose in the fall.

"Michelangelo must have smelled your fishy hair,"
Molly said, prying the cat from where it was lodged on
Daddy's shoulder.

"Fishy hair?" Daddy bristled. "My hair doesn't smell like
fish."

"Oh, yes, it does!" everyone called out.

"You stink!" added the lady in the red beret.

Naturally, I felt terrible that poor Sir Isaac had lost his nose, but part of me was secretly thrilled to see Daddy finally realize what a stink bomb he was.

In a rare display of humility, Daddy apologized to Lydia and Molly and offered to re-attach Sir Isaac's nose with Crazy Glue. After their somewhat icy refusal, he spotted me hiding in the corner and hustled me out the door—but not before grabbing one last cheese puff for the road.

I love him dearly, but the man is impossible!

XOXO,
Mom

To: Jausten
From: DaddyO
Subject: Minor Mishap

I suppose Mom's told you about the minor mishap at the Grand Unveiling last night. Frankly, I think Fig Newton looks much better without his nose, but that's just one man's highly artistic opinion.

And I don't see why everyone is blaming me. I wasn't the one who came sailing through the air to smell my hair. If you ask me, the whole thing is Michelangelo's fault.

But Mom may have been right about Big Al's Hair Wax. I went to the doctor this morning and discovered my sinuses were stuffed up. Thanks to a sinus rinse, they're all clear now. And when I took a whiff of Big Al's Hair Wax, I had to admit it did smell a bit fishy.

Love 'n hugs from,
DaddyO

PS. I've decided to give up sculpting, satisfied to have created my masterpiece, which I now have proudly displayed on a shelf in the garage, where Mom made me put it. True, from that vantage point it can't receive the accolades it deserves, but at least I get to appreciate it every time I park the Camry.

PPS. I don't care what Mom says; my Lady Liberty does *not* look like a gummy bear with a torch!

To: Jausten
From: Shoptillyoudrop
Subject: Begging and Groveling

Just got off the phone with Harvy, and after much begging and groveling, I got him to agree to see Daddy and get rid of his hideous haircut.

To: Jausten
From: DaddyO
Subject: Off To See Harvy

Dearest Lambchop—With heavy heart, I've agreed to give up my Metrosexual Mohawk. Which, I suppose, was inevitable. It doesn't look quite as striking without Big Al's Hair Wax to hold it in place.

**To: Jausten
From: Shoptillyoudrop
Subject: Bye-Bye, Mohawk!**

Daddy's back from his appointment with Harvy, who got rid of his moronic Mohawk. At last, he doesn't look like an aging extra in a punk rock video.

**To: Jausten
From: DaddyO
Subject: Fun While It Lasted**

I hated to lose my magnificent Mohawk, but I must admit, my new cut looks very good. Harvy really is a great haircutter.

Looking back on it, I can see how my daring do may have been a bit too wild for a man of my age (or any age, for that matter).

But it was fun while it lasted!

Love 'n snuggles
From your newly shorn,
DaddyO

**To: Jausten
From: Shoptillyoudrop
Subject: Life Is Good!**

Well, sweetheart, I'm happy to report all is well in Tampa Vistas. Daddy's given up sculpting. No fishy smell in the house. No stupid Statue of Liberty. And best of all, Sir Isaac's nose has been epoxied back on, and you can hardly notice the crack.

Life is good!

XOXO,
Mom

To: Jausten
From: DaddyO
Subject: Guess What Came in the Mail?

Great news, Lambchop! Guess what came in the mail? A discount coupon from Fast Eddie's House Painters. For a limited time only, Fast Eddie will paint a whole room in our house in just one day for a fraction of his usual rate.

Mom's been wanting to have the living room painted for the longest time. So I'm going to take her to St. Pete's for the day and surprise her with a freshly painted living room when we get back.

What's more, Fast Eddie is offering an extra discount on his discontinued paint colors. Which look darn good to me. I've chosen a lively Orange Popsicle. Just the splash of color our living room needs.

I can't wait to see the expression on Mom's face when she sees it!

Chapter 37

Daisy greeted me at the door when I showed up for work the next morning, looking a lot perkier than she had in recent days—her pixie cut freshly washed, gold hoops dangling from her ears, lips painted a bright pink.

"Jaine, dear! You're just the person I wanted to see. I've decided I absolutely must get out of my funk. And so I'm going to throw myself into *Fifty Shades*. In fact, I've come up with a few suggestions I'd like to toss your way."

Phooey-rats-darn-it-to-hell! I've been around the track more than a few times, and whenever a client tells me they've got "a few suggestions," it usually means a Page One Rewrite.

"I'll pop by your office in a bit to chat."

"Great!" I said, trying to sound as if I meant it.

After lobbing her a feeble wave good-bye, I dashed to the kitchen for a cup of coffee and a weensy chocolate croissant.

(Okay, it wasn't so weensy, but I was in crisis mode, and I needed all the chocolate I could get.)

Back in the office, I sank down into my chair with a sigh.

It seemed everything I'd been doing lately had been a waste of time. All that running around trying to find the killer for Kate, when all along it was probably Kate herself.

And now Daisy was going to waltz in with her "suggestions," which would no doubt undo all the blood, sweat, and heaving bosoms I'd poured into *Fifty Shades of Turquoise*.

It was no use working on the book until I heard what she had to say. So, after scarfing down my chocolate croissant, I checked my emails and read about Daddy's "minor mishap" at the art gallery. What a mess. Oh, well. At least "Fig" Newton's nose job had been a success.

Musing on Daddy's uncanny ability to create chaos wherever he goes, I absentmindedly picked up Dickie's creative energy crystal.

The pale blue rock rested in my palm like a misshapen ball. Idly I began tossing it back and forth, hoping it would give me the strength to deal with Daisy's new ideas.

There I was, playing catch with myself, when— oops!—I missed one of the tosses and the crystal went sailing into the framed photo on my desk, the one of Daisy as a toddler, sitting in her billionaire father's lap.

I gulped in dismay as the photo crashed onto the hardwood floor, glass shattering into what seemed like zillion shards.

When I got down on my knees to clean up the mess, I saw something odd. Very odd.

There, hidden behind the picture of Daisy and her dad, were three other photos. The first showed a clearly recognizable Daisy as a young woman. But this young woman was no heiress. Wearing a cheap cotton dress, she stood beside a rusted tractor with a man in overalls. Another picture was a school photo of Daisy from a high school in Hastings, Nebraska.

Hello. Didn't Kate say that Daisy had been raised in luxury on the East Coast? If so, what the heck had she been she doing going to Hastings High?

Then I picked up the third picture—a faded photo of Daisy standing with another woman, about her age and her size. But this other women was swathed in furs, while Daisy stood beside her in a simple wool coat.

I flashed back to the story Kate told me my first day at work, about Daisy's companion being killed in a tragic hiking accident.

Now, looking at these pictures, it occurred to me that maybe it was the other way around. The woman I knew as Daisy was never an heiress. The heiress was the one killed in Tuscany. Daisy was the *companion*!

Daisy must have somehow assumed her old boss's identity and had been living in luxury ever since.

Was it possible that Tommy knew about this switch and was blackmailing her? Is that why she'd been so kind to him, lavishing him with gifts, essentially turning over her fortune to him, all the while planning to bump him off?

So engrossed was I in this bombshell of a discovery, I failed to hear the sound of approaching footsteps.

"So now you know my little secret."

I looked up to see Daisy standing in the doorway, a steely glint in her normally placid blue eyes.

"You're not really Daisy Kincaid, are you?" I said.

"Nope," she shrugged. "Emma Shimmel from Hastings, Nebraska. I worked as the real Daisy's companion for twenty years. Twenty years of being treated like dirt, stuck with a sour old fossil of a boss.

"Absolutely loathed my job," she said, plopping down in Kate's chair and giving it a swivel. "But then one day I came up with a plan. It was so simple, really. Daisy liked taking nature walks. All I had to do was push her over a handy cliff and pawn it off as a tragic accident. The locals were only too happy to believe me, especially after I showered them with bribes. More cash got me a forged ID and passport. And voila, I became Daisy Kincaid!"

Beaming with pride, she continued her saga, eager to brag about how clever she'd been.

"Daisy was a recluse, never socializing, with few living relatives—all of them back east. So I packed my bags—I should say Daisy's bags—and moved to Los Angeles, where no one would have known the real Daisy."

For the first time a frown marred her cherubic face.

"What I never counted on was my own nephew showing up on my doorstep. From the time he was a little boy, Tommy had always been a manipulative little schemer."

Look who's talking! I felt like saying.

"He saw my picture in the *Bel Air Society News* and recognized me right away. He figured out my con and threatened to expose me unless I took him into my life and married him. There would have been a divorce, of course, with a giant settlement, and undoubtedly years of ensuing blackmail.

"I went along with it, pretending to be gaga over him, convincing everyone I was in love with him. So no one would ever dream I was the killer when I finally plunged that Swiss Army Knife in his neck.

"My, that was satisfying," she said, smiling at the memory. "What a pity you found those photos. Now we've got a bit of a problem."

She got up and made her way to the bookcase against the far wall, where she reached for a leather-bound copy of *Crime and Punishment*.

Was this one of her secret money stashes? Was she going to try bribing me to keep my mouth shut?

It was indeed a hollowed-out book, but when she opened it, I was horrified to see her whipping out a gun.

"These book safes are so handy!" she said, aiming the gun straight at my gut. "I'm afraid it's your turn to die, my dear."

Then she flicked a switch on the back of the bookcase, in the space where *Crime and Punishment* had been. The bookcase swung open, revealing a no-frills room stocked with bottled water, canned food, and a healthy supply of bourbon.

"My panic room." she grinned proudly.

So this was the panic room Solange told me about.

"The perfect place to hide your corpse!"

Now she trotted over to where I was standing frozen to the spot.

"Get moving," she said, prodding me in the back with her gun.

"You can't shoot me. Raymond and Solange will hear the gunshot."

"No, they won't. I gave them day off to make up for all the hell Tommy put them through. By the time they get back, you'll be long dead."

Another poke of steel in my back.

Oh, Lord, I thought, as she nudged me across the room to my own personal mausoleum. This was it. The end. Curtains. Just when I'd finally found true love, I was going to that great Oreo Factory in the Sky.

And what about Prozac? Tears stung my eyes. Who was going to feed her minced mackerel guts, give her belly rubs, and pick her hairballs out of their freshly washed laundry?

By now my pace had slowed to a crawl, anything to delay the inevitable.

And Emma was losing patience.

"Move it!" she shouted, ramming me with a shove that sent me stumbling to the ground.

And it was at that moment, when I'd pretty much given up hope, that I saw my salvation glittering in the morning sun—a stray shard of glass from the broken picture frame.

Pretending to struggle to my feet, I grabbed the glass and—with every ounce of strength I possessed—shoved it in Emma's leg. With a yelp of pain, she dropped her gun, which I wasted no time scooping up.

"Now it's your turn to get moving," I said, jumping up.

With the gun in her back, I nudged her the last few feet into the panic room.

"Jaine, dear!" Sweet as sugar. "Perhaps I acted a bit too rashly. I'm sure we can come to some sort of agreement. After all, I didn't do anything that bad. Not really. Daisy Kincaid was an unhappy woman. I put her out of her misery. And you have to agree I did the world a favor by getting rid of Tommy. Such a loathsome creature.

"What do you say?" she asked, as gaily as if she were inviting me for tea. "Let's make a deal. You keep my secret and I'll pay you a million dollars. That sounds fair, doesn't it?"

"To a sociopath, maybe, but not to me. I'm calling the police."

"It'll be your word against mine," she cried. "I'll show them the gash on my leg and tell them you tried to kill me."

"Nice try, Emma. But it's not going to work. I've got the pictures of the real you."

Indeed I did, having stashed them in my jeans pocket.

With that, I flicked the switch on the bookshelf and watched it swing shut.

"Don't even try to get out," I warned, "or I'll shoot you on sight."

"You miserable bitch!" she screamed from inside the panic room.

All traces of the gentle woman I'd known as Daisy were gone, replaced by a shrieking hellcat. Ignoring her stream of curses, I dug out my phone from my purse and called 911.

When the cops showed up, I opened the door to the panic room, where the former doyenne of La Belle Vie was slugging down bourbon straight from the bottle. I told them how Emma had confessed to killing both Daisy and Tommy. She denied everything, of course, once again playing the role of wide-eyed, ditsy Daisy Kincaid.

But the cops weren't buying it, not after I showed them the incriminating photos. Soon the phony heiress, her leg bandaged by a helpful police officer, was being whisked off to the county jail.

As the police led her out the door, she shot me a look of sheer malice, probably the same look she'd given the real Daisy before pushing her off that cliff.

"By the way, Jaine, you're fired. Finito. Cut off without another penny."

"So are you, Emma," I was happy to point out. "So are you."

I watched the police cart her away, grateful that the killer had been caught, justice had been served, and—most important—that there were still plenty of chocolate croissants left in the kitchen.

Chapter 38

I spent the next two days recuperating from my near-death experience, watching old movies with Prozac and pampering myself with restorative doses of Chunky Monkey.

Dickie stopped by to check up on me and bring me a vat of ghastly turnip soup.

"Isn't it delicious?" he asked as I gagged down a spoonful. "Hapi says it has amazing healing properties."

For a minute, I was tempted to tell him about the Hapi hamburger incident, but I couldn't bear to burst his bubble. So I said nothing, forcing down a few more spoonfuls of soup.

Unfortunately, Dickie's visit was cut short by Pro's constant hissing from her perch on my bedspread.

Who invited HIM?

"So sorry she's being impossible," I sighed.

"Not a problem," Dickie assured me. "But I want you to bring her with you when you come to dinner at my condo."

"Are you sure about that?" I asked, picturing his condo in shambles, FEMA guys picking their way through the rubble.

"Absolutely," he said. "Cats are very territorial. I think she'll feel far less threatened by me at my place.

"And besides," he added, "I've got a very special gift waiting for her—and an even more special gift waiting for you."

"Gift? What gift?"

"You'll find out on Saturday," he winked before kissing me good-bye and heading back to Venice.

Hmm. What special gift had Dickie bought me? I wondered as I tossed his soup down the garbage disposal. Could it possibly be an engagement ring? Was Dickie going to propose? Were we about to get married in a romantic beachfront ceremony, saying our "I do's" with a glorious sunset as our backdrop?

Whoa, I cautioned myself, tamping down my hopes. It was probably another creative energy crystal or a gift certificate to a spin class.

But in spite of my best efforts to rein myself in, visions of engagement rings continued to dance in my head in the days leading up to our dinner.

At last the big night arrived. I spiffed myself up in my best skinny jeans and black cashmere turtleneck, my hair semi-straightened into a tousled bedhead look, my feet clad in my one and only pair of Manolos.

Needless to say, Prozac was her usual sunny self as I tried to get her into her carrier.

Unhand me this minute! What do you think you're doing? Keep this up and I'm going to report you to the ASPCA! The ACLU! The CIA! Nothing will stop me in my pursuit of justice—Hey, do I smell savory salmon innards?

She lunged at the kitty treat I'd tossed in the carrier, and I snapped the latch shut.

Then I set off for Dickie's condo, praying the fur wouldn't fly once we got there.

Dickie was looking particularly yummy that night in chinos and a striped Oxford shirt, his sun-streaked hair smelling of citrus shampoo. I, on the other hand, looked more than a tad frazzled due to twenty-five minutes of nonstop yowling from Prozac on the drive over.

"Look what I got you, Pro," Dickie said as I opened the door to her carrier and she came whooshing out. "A litter box."

He pointed with a flourish to a litter box he'd set up in the foyer.

Prozac gave it a dismissive sniff.

Wow. My very own toilet. What a thrill.

"That's very sweet of you, Dickie," I said. "But all the same, I'm glad you've got hardwood floors. I don't trust Prozac to behave herself."

"I'm sure she'll be a perfect angel, won't you, Pro?" Dickie cooed.

I fully expected her to poop on the floor just to get on his nerves, but much to my surprise, she actually purred when he bent down to scratch her.

"See?" Dickie said. "I knew she'd warm up to me here in the condo."

Maybe he was right. Maybe outside my apartment, Prozac would learn to love him.

"And look what else I got you, Pro!" he said, leading the way into his stainless steel and granite counter kitchen, where he took a jar from the counter and put it down in front of her

"Caviar!" Dickie beamed.

Another dismissive sniff from her ladyship.

Domestic.

But she swan dived into it anyway, inhaling the stuff at lightning speed.

"Just let me heat up our lasagna," Dickie said. "Then we'll go out to the balcony to watch the sunset.

"Lasagna?" My taste buds sprang to life. "We're having lasagna for dinner?"

"Yes, indeedie," he said with a highly kissable grin. "I know how much you like it."

How sweet! Dickie had put aside Hapi's ban on pasta just to please me!

I was on culinary cloud nine as he poured us each a glass of organic chardonnay to take out to the balcony. Passing the dining area, I noticed the table set with spotless linens and a bowl of lilacs as a centerpiece.

"Lilacs!" I exclaimed. "My favorite flower!"

"I remember," Dickie said. "That why I got them."

Then, not a moment too soon, he took me in his arms and zeroed in for that kiss I'd been hankering for.

This was usually the point where Prozac erupted in a hissy fit, but she seemed mercifully uninterested in our smooching, instead wandering down the hallway toward Dickie's bedroom.

Out on the balcony, Dickie and I sat cuddled together on a chaise, Dickie telling me about the latest developments on his ad campaign, me not really paying attention. I was too busy thinking about that lasagna—and my "special gift."

Once again, I tried to tamp down my expectations. I thought of all the dreadful gifts Dickie had given me when we were married—the used tool belt, the toaster with crumbs still inside, the *Happy Bat Mitzvah, Kimberly!* flowers he'd picked from the neighbor's trash.

True, Dickie had turned over a new leaf since those days—witness the lilacs and the lasagna—but I couldn't allow my hopes to soar too high.

The sun having set in a glorious ball of orange, we polished off our wine and went back inside the condo. The minute I stepped over the threshold I stopped dead in my tracks.

The place reeked to high heaven, a god-awful stench that had to have rivaled Big Al's Hair Wax on the Stink-o-meter.

"What's that smell?" I gasped.

"Cabbage!" Dickie grinned. "For our cabbage lasagna!"

"Cabbage lasagna?"

"One of Hapi's most popular recipes. You use cabbage leaves instead of pasta to separate the layers of chopped veggie filling."

At which point, my taste buds lapsed into a deep coma.

"Wait right here," Dickie said, leading me to my seat at the dining table before scooting off to the kitchen.

Alone at the table, I leaned into the lilacs, taking deep breaths, hoping to drown out the cabbage stench. But it was no use. Those poor lilacs didn't stand a chance against Hapi's cabbage lasagna.

I was sitting there wondering how I was ever going to

get used to Hapi's reign of terror in the kitchen when I saw something that made the whole world smell good again.

It was Dickie, walking over to me—with a Tiffany gift bag!

"I was going to give this to you after dessert, but I couldn't wait. Here," he said, handing it to me.

"Omigosh!" I gasped. "Tiffany!"

Then I felt a quick stab of fear. The used tool belt he'd given me had been wrapped in a box from Bloomingdale's. Would I reach into the bag only to find a cheese grater with shards of cheddar still stuck to it?

Somewhat hesitantly, I riffled through the tissue paper until I came to a small box at the bottom.

A ring box!

I opened it to find a honker of a diamond winking up at me.

Holy moly! Dickie had come through with an actual ring from Tiffany!

And what a ring. I was no expert, but this thing had to be a couple of carats.

"It's gorgeous," I said, lifting it out from the box and slipping it on my finger.

I knew Dickie was doing well at his new job, but had no idea he was doing diamonds-from-Tiffany well.

"Can you really afford this? It must have cost a fortune."

"Nothing's too good for my Jaine! So what do you say?" he asked, getting down on one knee. "Will you—"

But he never got a chance to finish that thought, because just then the oven timer dinged.

"The lasagna!" he said, springing up. "Be right back!"

He dashed off to the kitchen, leaving me in a happy glow.

Dickie wanted to marry me!

Not only that, he'd given me the engagement ring of my dreams.

I watched it twinkling like a zillion stars, then took it off to admire the band.

It was then that I saw something written on the inside of the ring.

How sweet! He'd even had it inscribed!

Wondering what words of love he'd chosen, I read the inscription. And was boggled to see:

For Carmelita, Ay Caramba!

What the what? Who the heck was Carmelita?

Then the dawn came. He'd done it again. Another re-cycled gift. It was the used tool belt, the crumb-filled toaster, and Kimberly's Bat Mitzvah flowers all over again.

Dickie hadn't changed.

He may have had a new job and condo, but underneath it all, he was still the same old Dickie I'd divorced.

At which point, he came trotting back to the room.

"Now where was I?" he said, getting down on one knee.

I swatted away his hand as it reached for mine.

"Who, may I ask, is Carmelita?"

"Carmelita?" He blinked, puzzled. "I don't know any Carmelita."

"Then why is her name engraved on my engagement ring?"

I showed him the inscription, and he blushed with guilt.

"You didn't really get this ring at Tiffany, did you?"

"No," he admitted. "I bought it off a guy at a taco stand. But he swore it was a genuine cubic zirconia."

The Blob was back, all right. A lying, scheming sack of poo.

I didn't care that it wasn't a diamond. (Well, not much, anyway.) I just cared that he lied.

"Anything else you'd like to come clean about?" I asked.

As if on cue, Prozac—in a moment she'd no doubt been longing for—came prancing in to join us, a red valet parker's vest dangling from her mouth.

She dropped it at my feet, bursting with pride.

Look what I just found!

So Lance really did see The Blob parking cars at a restaurant!

"You work as a valet parker?"

He nodded, sheepish.

No wonder he was always busy at night.

"Your ad job? Does that even exist?"

"Not really," he confessed.

"I don't get it," I said. "How can you afford this condo and a BMW working as a valet parker?"

I was about to find out.

Because just then we heard the front door opening and footsteps in the foyer.

We hurried over to see a tall, dark-haired guy wheeling in a suitcase.

Dickie blanched at the sight of him.

"Mark! What are you doing here? You're not due back from London until next week."

"I know, but Chrissy got the flu and we took an earlier flight home."

At which point, a gorgeous blonde joined him, the same gorgeous blonde whose photo I'd seen in the night table drawer.

"Thanks so much for housesitting, pal," Mark said as he shuffled off his jacket.

"What's that awful smell?" Chrissy asked, wrinkling her nose.

"Cabbage lasagna!" Dickie said. "Want some? The recipe serves eight."

"Ugh, no!" Chrissy groaned.

"Mark and Chrissy own the restaurant I work for," Dickie said, turning to me. "I was housesitting for them while they were in London opening a new restaurant."

"So I'm guessing you don't really drive a BMW?"

"You drove my BMW?" Mark asked, clearly annoyed. "You were only supposed to start up the engine so the battery wouldn't die."

A shamefaced shrug from Dickie.

"So where do you actually live?" I asked.

"With a group of Hapi-ness members in an apartment in Glendale. I'm sorry I haven't been entirely truthful."

"Entirely truthful? You've been lying like a time share salesman in the Gobi Desert."

"Only because I love you, and also because we're losing the lease on the apartment in Glendale. I was hoping I'd be able to move in with you. I realize I'm not perfect, but as Hapi has taught me, I forgive myself for my imperfections."

"Well, I don't!" I said, hurling his stupid ring at him. "We're done, Dickie!"

"In that case, would you mind reimbursing me for the caviar?"

I didn't even dignify that with a response.

"C'mon, Pro," I said. "We're outta here."

Picking her up from where she was perched on Dickie's valet vest, I saw she'd adorned it with a decorative piece of poop.

Prozac looked up at Dickie, her big green eyes twinkling merrily.

My parting gift to you.

"Ugh!" Dickie groaned, wrinkling his nose. "That smells disgusting!"

"Not as bad as the cabbage," Chrissy pointed out.

"Amen to that," I said, grabbing Prozac's carrier and storming out the door.

"Oh, Pro!" I said out in the hallway. "You were magnificent!"

I giggled at the memory of her poop on Dickie's vest.

And as I headed for the elevator, I felt a weight lift from my shoulders. How wonderful it was to be free again. No more pretending to like spin classes. Or Hapi's hellish diet. Or Dickie's silly affirmations.

Prozac had been right about him all along.

"So what should I order for dinner?" I asked my sagacious kitty. "Chinese? Pizza? Deli?"

She beamed up at me from where she was nestled in my arm.

Sounds good. And what will you be having?

HEADLINES IN THE NEWS

Convicted murderer Emma Shimmel inks $500,000 movie deal for Fifty Shades of Turquoise. Sizzling romance to star newcomer Solange Delacroix as "Clarissa Weatherly."

***

Marty "Hapi" Mellman, New Age guru and owner of The Body Shop strip club, sentenced to ten years for money laundering.

***

Esme Larkin, Clayton Manning to Wed at Bel Air Tennis Club.

***

Saudi prince buys famed mansion, La Belle Vie, for trysts with stripper Misty Harbor.

***

Gourmet chef draws crowds with spuds: Los Angelenos line around the block for Raymond's House of Tater Tots.

Please turn the page for an exciting sneak peek at
Laura Levine's next Jaine Austen mystery
MURDER GETS A MAKEOVER
coming soon wherever print and e-books are sold!

I never should have agreed to that makeover. If only I'd stayed true to my elastic waist pants and ketchup-stained sweats, I wouldn't have wound up with a murder rap hanging over my head.

On the day it all began I was at my computer, trying to churn out a brochure for Toiletmasters Plumbers, extolling the virtues of their double-flush commode.

But it wasn't easy. Not with my cat Prozac perched on my window sill, hissing like an asthmatic radiator.

The object of her rancor was a particularly bushy-tailed squirrel scampering up a nearby palm tree. Prozac had been fixated on this critter for the past several days, going bonkers whenever she saw it.

"Prozac," I snapped, after staring at my blinking cursor for fifteen minutes. "Stop that hissing right now!"

Ever cooperative, she stopped hissing. And started yowling instead.

"What is it with you?" I groaned. "It's just a squirrel."

She tore her eyes away from the window just long enough to shoot me a withering glare.

Just a squirrel? Can't you see it's an evil alien from the Planet Acorn, out to destroy democracy as we know it? Only I can save the planet from total doom!

What can I say? My cat's delusional. I didn't name her Prozac for nothing.

So there I was, slaving away on Toiletmasters' double flush commode, wondering if I could trade Prozac in for a goldfish, when my neighbor Lance came knocking at my front door.

"I've got fabulous news!" he gushed, sailing into my apartment in a designer suit, his blond curls moussed to perfection. "Bebe Braddock wants to give you a fashion makeover!"

"Bebe who?" I asked, puzzled.

"Bebe Braddock, stylist to the stars! She dresses all the "A" list Hollywood celebrities and she's one of my most loyal customers at Neiman's!"

The Neiman's to which he referred was the famed department store, Neiman Marcus, where Lance is gainfully employed as a shoe salesman, fondling the tootsies of the rich and famous.

"Bebe wants to do a Before & After makeover on her Instagram page, and I convinced her to use you! I told her what a fashion disaster you were!"

"Did you now? How very thoughtful."

As usual, my sarcasm soared over his blond curls.

"No need to thank me, hon. That's what friends are for. Anyhow, I showed her a picture of you in your *Cuckoo for Cocoa Puffs* t-shirt, and she can't wait to turn you from frumpy to fabulous."

"For your information, I happen to like the way I dress. It's California Casual."

"Only if you're dumpster diving in Malibu. Seriously, Jaine. There are vultures circling over our duplex, waiting for your clothes to die."

"Forget it. No way am I giving up my elastic waist pants and cutting off the free flow of calories from my lips to my hips."

Lance shook his head in disgust.

"I can't believe you're passing up this golden opportunity."

He looked down at Prozac, who'd abandoned her yowling to slither around his ankles.

"She's crazy, isn't she, Pro?"

Prozac purred in agreement.

I'll say. She doesn't even believe in evil aliens from the Planet Acorn.

Lance took off in a cloud of disapproval, and the minute he was gone, Prozac resumed her perch on the windowsill, yowling her little head off.

Seeking refuge from the din, I headed out to the supermarket to stock up on fruits and vegetables. (Okay, peanut butter and Double Stuf Oreos.)

I drove over, still steaming at Lance. The nerve of that guy. Calling me a fashion disaster.

My thoughts about Lance were put on hold, however, when I pulled into the parking lot and saw a bunch of teenagers tossing empty soda cans into the trash. How irresponsible, when there was a clearly marked bin for recyclables right next to it.

Now I happen to care about the planet almost as much

as I care about Double Stuf Oreos. So I marched over and started retrieving the cans from the trash. Unfortunately they were at the bottom of the bin, and I had to bend over quite a bit to reach them.

I was trying to fish them out when I felt someone tap me on the shoulder.

I turned around to see a distinguished old gent in tweeds and tasseled loafers.

"Here, my dear," he said, holding out a twenty dollar bill. "Use this to buy yourself something to eat. And bus fare to a homeless shelter."

Good heavens! He thought I was homeless.

"No, you don't understand, sir. I was just trying to re-cycle."

"This is no time for foolish pride, young lady. Take the money and get yourself a hot meal. Maybe stop off at Goodwill for a change of clothing, too."

I stood there, dazed, as he walked away. And for the first time that day, I took a good look at my outfit.

I flushed, ashamed, when I realized I could play connect-the-dots with the ketchup stains on my sweats.

Maybe Lance was right. Maybe it was time to update my look.

So I took out my cell and called him.

"Hey, Lance," I said when he picked up. "It's me, Jaine."

And then I uttered those fateful words I'd soon live to regret:

"I think I'll try that makeover after all."